Laurie Brady is a published poet, a writer of short stories, a novelist, and a great dog lover who lives in Sydney, Australia. He has a keen sense of humour, particularly a liking for the ridiculous, and a love of literature and sport. He has spent most of his working life as a teacher and a teacher educator, promoting engaging and quality schooling. He retired recently as professor of education at the University of Technology, Sydney.

To Brady, Georgia, Kayla, Lachlan and Joshua, and to dog lovers everywhere.

Laurie Brady

ENTER SPICE

AUSTIN MACAULEY PUBLISHERS™

LONDON · CAMBRIDGE · NEW YORK · SHARJAH

A CIP catalogue record for this title is available from the British Library.

ISBN 9781398444850 (Paperback)
ISBN 9781398446885 (ePub e-book)

www.austinmacauley.com

First Published 2022
Austin Macauley Publishers Ltd®
1 Canada Square
Canary Wharf
London
E14 5AA

Chapter 1

Sometimes people see the weather as a sign. A hot and sunny blue day is a sign of good things to come. All is well with the world. But a wet and miserable day may mean that everything is not going to be alright. Or if there is a storm, with lightning and thunder, it might be a sign that something big has happened, or is about to happen.

There had just been a furious storm. The thunder sounded as if the world was breaking apart, and lightning knifed the sky in jagged cuts. It was now raining steadily, lashing the windows, and a wind was blowing like a shrill note on a recorder.

Tom Ellis, now in his late forties, had reason to believe the weather was a sign. He'd just lost his dog Donegal, his close companion of many years, and was feeling very sad. He loved his family, but felt as though a large part of his life had crumbled away to nothing.

Donegal had been no ordinary dog. He'd been with the Ellis family for three years before he suddenly, without warning, revealed to Tom that he could walk and run upright like people, talk, write, and play sports. He had become more than a family pet. He helped Tom's two children, Scott and Lara, with their homework, he played with them each afternoon, he rescued children and other dogs from harm, and his advice to all members of the family was always proven to be correct or wise.

Donegal had a good idea of how long a dog might live. It wasn't as long as people. It was often said that one year for people is the same as seven years for dogs. So, after a few years, he had stopped walking upright, talking, writing and playing human's games with Scott and Lara. He returned to being a normal dog, sleeping in a kennel, eating his kibble and a raw bone, and he had wandered away at nights after his walk with Tom. He had announced that it was time he started to help other dogs.

A few years passed and Donegal resisted all the attempts of the family to have him return to the almost human dog that he once was. Tom's wife Beth was secretly pleased that Donegal had returned to being only a dog. She hadn't been sure how she should behave towards a dog who was as much a man as a dog. She found it hard to pat and stroke him when he was standing upright, and was as tall as she was.

Scott and Lara wanted him to be the celebrity he once was, because it made them celebrities too. He was always on television and in the newspapers. They couldn't understand why he was a mere dog again. They thought like most people that Donegal had suffered some sort of medical problem that had changed him. Something like a stroke. Perhaps it was the hand of God. Some people said it was God's way of restoring the natural order of the world.

In time, the family's disappointment became acceptance. They weren't children anymore, and it had been some time since they'd played with him after school. They'd grown older, and had developed other interests. Donegal was still very much loved, but he wasn't the centre of their lives as he had once been.

Scott still lived at home, but was twenty-one, and had a girlfriend, Tiffany, with whom he spent a lot of time. She was well liked by the family. Lara was nineteen, and at university studying to be a vet.

Tom had been aware of the signs of ageing in Donegal. Even he complained of the arthritis in his back from running upright, and the hint of grey around his snout. The others hadn't noticed, so his death had come as a complete surprise and shock. For them, there had been no warning.

They were all terribly upset, but the night of the storm, Beth, Scott and Lara had been convinced that they should go to the show that Beth had bought very expensive tickets for weeks earlier. It might cheer us up a bit, she'd told them, though she only half believed it. But when it came time to go, Tom couldn't. The thought of enjoying himself just didn't seem right. He was hurting too much, and going out wasn't going to help. He would make the others even more miserable. So, Tiffany was given his ticket and Tom found himself alone in the house at night.

He was desperately lonely, but didn't want to be with anyone. When the storm arrived, he'd been moving from room to room. He was so restless, he couldn't sit still in one place for more than a few minutes. The lights were off. He didn't want them on. They lit up too many memories. There were enough of them without lights. The time Donegal first spoke and went upright to make the coffee. The time he rescued the little girl from drowning and lay exhausted on the beach. The time he returned home with thirty dogs he'd set free from the council pound. The time he single-handed or single-pawed, captured the burglars trying to rob them. The time he told the woman enrolling students at the university that there was no rule excluding dogs from being students. And there were memories of Donegal in every room of the house.

Yes, the weather was a sign, Tom thought. It meant something huge had happened. Enough for the heavens to cry out. But even recalling these funny memories, Tom couldn't smile. The pain was too great.

The thunder and lightning had stopped, but it was raining heavily. He was sitting in the family room when he heard a scratching sound coming from the back door. It was probably a small tree branch blown against the door and being agitated by the howling wind.

When the tapping continued and became louder, Tom went to investigate. It was black beyond the glass door, but he could make out something that wasn't a branch. It was round and it moved, obviously an animal of some sort. The glass was foggy. He opened the door carefully and let in a wet and shivering cocker spaniel.

She stood on the tiled entrance, not daring to shake herself, the way dogs usually do. He'd later learn this was because she didn't want to spray rain water over the carpet and furniture.

'I'll get a towel,' he said aloud to himself, and turned to go to the laundry.

'I'm Spice,' the dog said in a gentle female voice. 'Terrible weather isn't it?'

Tom turned around quickly and stared. He was stunned. Spice stared back and smiled.

Then it was Tom's turn to smile. 'Oh Donegal,' he said softly, and he turned his face from Spice so that she wouldn't see his tears. It was clear that her coming must have had something to do with Donegal. He was silent for half a minute, unable to act or to say anything more.

'Now about that towel,' Spice reminded him. She was still shivering, and Tom, having suddenly remembered where he was, and turning again for the laundry, surprised himself by saying, 'Sorry Spice.'

When he returned with the towel, Spice took it from him and dried herself, paying particular attention to her paws. She didn't want to wet or dirty the floor. Her fur, once it was dried and fluffed-up, gained colour, and showed itself to be a chocolate brown with patches of white. She had honey-coloured eyes, and a soft white snout or nose. The twinkle in her eyes reminded him of Donegal.

He felt excited and also sad, a real porridge of feelings. He'd felt so good when she'd spoken to him. The pain he was feeling had eased. He didn't know if she was here to stay. Even after only a few minutes, he hoped she was. At the same time, he didn't want to feel that she was taking Donegal's place. He didn't want to feel that it was like a betrayal, that Donegal was easy to be replaced. But if her being here was Donegal's doing, then it's what Donegal would want, what she and Donegal had agreed to.

He didn't know what to say or do. Where to start? What had she known of Donegal? Could she walk upright? She walked in the house on all four legs. Did she have a knowledge of almost everything you could find on the internet? What were her other talents? And how could she possibly have known of Donegal's death only a matter of hours ago?

He settled for a simple beginning. 'Can I get you a drink?' he asked. 'Perhaps a hot drink? Do you like tea, coffee, chocolate or just hot milk?' Then, thinking he might be expecting too much of Spice's abilities, he added, 'I can give you Donegal's old drinking bowl if you prefer.'

'I'd love a cup of tea,' she answered, 'and a cup is fine,' and as Tom was boiling the kettle, he saw her yawn, holding a paw to cover her mouth. She was sitting on the carpet and her head was dropping as if she was about to fall asleep.

'I beg your pardon,' she said. 'I don't mean to be rude. It has been a very long day.'

'We have so much to talk about,' Tom answered, but he could see she was tired and needed to rest. 'When you've finished your tea, you must sleep. The family will be home soon, and I'm sure we'll all have a thousand questions for you tomorrow.'

'Thanks Tom,' Spice answered as if they'd been friends for years. She already knew his name though he hadn't given it. 'If it's alright with you, I'll just curl up here on the floor…'

'Nonsense,' Tom said gently. 'You'll do no such thing.' He was overcoming his original shock, and already warming to the new visitor. 'There's a bed for you upstairs…but I think you might already know that.' He put the towel back in the laundry, and showed Spice to the spare room. He observed how she climbed the stairs on all four feet. There were so many questions to ask. So much he didn't know.

She'd only been gone for a few minutes when the family arrived home. They were exhausted, tired from the travel in driving rain, and tired from the day's emotion.

'Are you alright Tom?' Beth asked, hurrying over to hold him. 'We were all so worried about you alone at a time like this. It was probably a mistake to go. I don't think any of us could concentrate.'

Tom nodded and smiled. 'I'm OK,' he said, aware of Beth looking at him curiously.

The family said their 'good nights', went straight to bed and slept soundly, except for Tom. His mind was racing with a thousand thoughts and feelings. What could Spice do? She could speak, but could she read, write, walk upright, or play sports? Did she have some or all of the talents Donegal had?

What could she tell them about her relationship with Donegal? Would the others welcome her?

He was out of bed early in the morning because he thought it was important he have time to prepare the family for Spice's appearance. They might think it strange to have a dog they'd never seen before wandering around the house. He was careful not to wake the others as he knocked quietly and entered Spice's room to explain this to her. She was already awake and making the bed.

He asked her how she'd slept, and then asked the question that had kept him awake for most of the night, 'Will you be staying? I mean…' He swallowed. 'I'm not sure what to tell the others. I'm not even sure what they'll think. Would you like to be a part of our family?'

'I was hoping you'd ask,' she answered. 'I'd like that very much,' and looked at him steadily with her soft brown eyes. 'As long as you or the others don't think it's too soon, I mean too soon after Donegal.'

'I'm sure everyone will be delighted,' Tom said, and the matter was settled.

While Spice stayed in her room, Tom called the puzzled family together. 'I was fast asleep,' Scott moaned. 'We haven't even had breakfast yet,' said Lara. But they all knew that Tom had taken Donegal's death very badly, even worse than they had, and they didn't want to upset him further. They thought he had reached a decision about how to deal with their loss. He needed to talk, even if it were just to share his feelings. So, they sat together in their pyjamas in the family room and waited patiently for him to speak.

Tom came straight to the point. 'What do you think about having another dog?' he began. They were confused. It was not what they had expected, and he seemed restless and pleased. They'd expected him to be miserable, suggesting some tribute or celebration of Donegal's life. Wasn't it too soon to be thinking of another pet.

'We don't have to be in such a hurry dear,' Beth said soothingly.

'Not after Donegal,' Scott answered.

'We could never find a dog to replace him,' Lara agreed.

'But what if he…or she, was just like Donegal.' Tom was not disturbed by Scott and Lara's reaction. He was looking pleased, and without waiting for an answer, he looked towards the stairs and called 'Spice.' It was like introducing the star performer onto the stage, only the 'Ladies and Gentlemen' introduction and a roll of drums was missing.

The family followed his look, and after a few seconds, Spice walked upright down the stairs, smiling, her eyes shining. Their mouths fell open and they stared. Lara lost her balance and had to climb back onto the lounge.

'What the…' Scott began and was silent.

'I hope you don't mind,' Spice said, her first words for the family, 'but I used the brush on the dressing table. Perhaps it was yours Lara?' She looked pretty, and for the first time, Tom noticed her long eyelashes.

'I don't believe it.' Beth was the first to speak, her eyes popping out of her head.

'It's like history repeating itself,' Scott said amazed, thinking of Donegal.

'But she's beautiful,' Lara said, looked embarrassed and apologised. 'I mean, you're beautiful,' and she looked at Spice and blushed.

'Spice would be happy to be one of our family,' Tom said, pleased with how things had started, 'but only if we all agree.'

There was an immediate chorus. 'Wonderful.'

'Of course.'

'Great.'

And there was no need for introductions, because Spice knew who each of them was, and said hello to them all in turn.

They all had a thousand questions for her, and it soon became apparent that she was well liked by everyone. Beth was delighted and sat on the lounge with her, leaning against her and holding her paw. Spice was a girl and much shorter than Donegal. She wasn't a half-human male as tall as Beth.

Lara competed with Scott in asking for information. They were questions about how she'd known Donegal, and whether she had the same talents. Lara thought of how Spice might help when she was working as a vet. Scott already liked Spice a lot, and couldn't wait to phone Tiffany with the news. He knew she'd be delighted.

The family understood, without Tom saying anything, that Spice wasn't just replacing Donegal. Her arrival must have been arranged by Donegal. She wasn't there by chance. It was surely what he'd wanted, and he must have known that it would help them from feeling so much pain at his own loss. Their grief at losing him was therefore softened by the arrival of Spice, and by his generous consideration.

'If it's alright with you Spice,' Tom said in front of the family, 'we'll keep your special talents a secret, whatever they are, at least for a while. We need time to think about how to let people know.' Everyone agreed. It was already obvious that Spice didn't want to be famous.

'A secret except for Tiffany,' Scott insisted.

'And perhaps your neighbour,' Spice added. 'Mrs Grouse, is it?' The family laughed. 'Rouse,' they said together. 'I was told it might be wise to become friends with her.'

*

The next few weeks were enjoyable for everyone. Spice came to know the four family members, though she seemed to already have a full understanding of them. She knew what each of them liked to do, what they liked to eat and drink, what they liked on television, and she knew what little things might please and upset each of them.

And the family grew in understanding of her. They learned that she could not only talk, but she could read and write. She could run fast on two legs, and while she could play most sports reasonably well, she wasn't a real star as Donegal had been. Her height and strength were disadvantages. She could draw and sing beautifully like Donegal, and play violin and piano. She also had the gift of speaking in different voices, and copying how others spoke.

While Donegal had perfect manners, Spice ate more slowly and with more delicacy. She spoke more softly, and her laugh was like a little tinkling bell rather than like Donegal's gravelly belly laugh.

Because she was so small, only coming up to Beth's hips when standing on two legs, there were things she couldn't reach. But after a few days, Tom made some steps she could use to open the fridge, help Beth with the cooking, and see herself in her dressing table mirror.

She spent the same amount of time with each family member, and with Tiffany who she met the same day as the others. Tiffany quickly developed the same bond with Spice that she had enjoyed with Donegal.

Tom had been the only one to take Donegal on his night time run. No one dared to take Tom's place. But now, Beth insisted on sharing the responsibility of running with Spice, and soon became her main running companion. 'It's a conspiracy,' Tom said when he saw them going off together, but he was always laughing.

Two weeks after Spice's arrival, Tom was digging up a small tree that had been planted where there was too much sun. Its leaves were curling and going yellow. He was going to plant it in a shady place, and was being careful not to damage the roots.

'Tom, oh Tom!' Beth's voice called from the kitchen window. 'There's a man here, who says you backed into his car in the Woolworths' car park. He's not very happy and wants money. Please come.'

Tom felt very concerned. His car had been scratched, even dented a few times. And no one ever left their contact details. The parking spots were so small and many people were not honest. It was hard to open the door to climb in and out. Perhaps he had bumped another car without even knowing it. So, he put down his spade and moved slowly to the house, worried and not knowing what to expect. It would be another expense. The man might be hostile, looking for a fight.

'Where is he?' he asked Beth, who had just entered the kitchen.

'Where's who?' Beth answered, looking surprised.

'The man about the car.'

'What car, and what man Tom? You're not making sense.'

They stood facing each other for a few seconds, before they heard Beth's voice again. 'Have you been a naughty boy Tom?' But it wasn't Beth. It was Spice who was speaking, imitating Beth.

Tom and Beth had to laugh. 'Who's the naughty one Spice Ellis,' Tom replied, happier now and giving her the name and therefore the status of a full member of the family.

'Sorry Tom, but it was time for a break,' Spice grinned, offering him a lemonade that he had to reach down to accept.

A few days later, Tom and Beth watched from the kitchen window, as Bruno, a dark brown kelpie from somewhere across the paddock was showing an interest in Spice. Bruno was a frequent and not welcome visitor to the Ellis house, because he dug holes at the base of trees, damaging their roots, and tore up flowers. And he left his business on the lawn for people to step on. Tom had often tried to shoo him away but he kept coming back. Now Spice might be another reason for him to come.

Spice was walking on four legs, and they were circling each other. Beth was about to ask Tom to go out and rescue Spice, or shoo Bruno away, when the two dogs stopped and for several seconds were face to face before Spice stood upright.

Tom could see Bruno's hair standing on end, and his head tilted as if he was listening. Suddenly he turned and raced away yelping as if he were being chased by a pack of wolves. Spice walked slowly back to the house.

'What was that all about?' Beth asked.

'Are you OK?' Tom added.

Spice smiled. 'I told him I was a dog by day, and a human at night, and I was being punished for doing bad things.'

*

The neighbour, Mrs Rouse was an old woman now. She lived alone and had become fat. She had enjoyed some fame when Donegal had given dogs a home in her house while she was away. She had been furious when she discovered the mess they left, and was determined to cause big trouble for Tom, but when the television and newspapers praised her for being an animal lover, she changed her story. And she'd put herself forward as Donegal's best friend. It was a story she told every visitor and every tradesman.

She didn't really care for animals at all. Pets were too much trouble. They had to be fed, exercised, and they left fur on the lounges. Some of them had accidents in the house. So, when she saw a tan and white cocker spaniel at the back door, she raised her arm to shoo it away. 'Out, out!' she called. 'I've had enough of your kind.'

Spice went back home, but even though Mrs Rouse had been very rude, she was determined to become her friend. So, with Beth's help, she made some scones, filled little containers with strawberry jam and cream, and returned to Mrs. Rouse's.

This time, she stood on two legs at the back door, and when Mrs. Rouse answered, rubbing her eyes as though she couldn't believe what she was seeing, Spice held out the plate of scones, and said very gently, 'Hello Mrs. Rouse. My name is Spice. I live next door. I've heard that you have been very kind to many of my friends.'

Mrs Rouse didn't know what to say or do. She was torn between sending Spice away, or letting her in. She was a pretty little dog, not rough looking, and so polite. There was nothing threatening about her.

'You'd better come in,' she said, taking the plate from Spice. 'Do you want to sit down. I mean on a chair... or on the... Will you have a scone yourself?'

So, they sat down at the kitchen table, eating the scones, and chatting. This was a new experience for Mrs. Rouse. She'd never liked animals much, and here she was telling a dog her life history, about her childhood dream of being a dancer, and about her long dead husband Reg and their children. She was enjoying herself more than she had for years. Very few people were interested in hearing her talk.

She knew she was seen as a grumpy old woman, and began to imagine Spice being a part of her life, and living in the same house. There was so much they could share.

When it was time for Spice to go, Mrs Rouse asked her if she would come again and soon, and reached out to pat the top of her head. She later worried if that had been the right thing to do. You don't pat people on the head…or tickle them behind the ears.

What is it about that Ellis family, she sighed.

Chapter 2

'Let's hear what the ad says,' Tom replied when Beth said she might apply for the job of Mr Dalton's personal assistant. 'Then we can tell if it suits you.' Beth had been doing some work at 'Dalton and Groves' for a few years, and thought she was ready for more demanding work. Most of what she was doing didn't challenge her brain. Lara, her youngest, had now left school and was at university learning to be a vet. So, both her children were now able to look after themselves. They didn't need to be driven to dance, sport or music lessons anymore. They didn't need baby-sitters if she and Tom went out.

'It doesn't say much,' Beth answered. The position will be filled by someone inside the organisation, and she began to read from the paper that had been given to all the workers at 'Dalton and Groves' that afternoon. *'A position is available for personal secretary to Mr Dalton. The successful applicant will assist Mr Dalton in all aspects of the senior partner's work including answering the phone, making appointments, organising interviews and social occasions, attending to the payment of workers, and arranging Mr Dalton's work schedule on a daily and weekly basis. The successful applicant will need to have excellent skills of organisation, and the ability to get along with others. She, or he will have*

*to be reliable and trustworthy, and have a record of efficiency
with the company.'*

'You'd be good at all those things,' Tom said. 'You must
apply for it. You need the challenge.'

'But there are others who've been with the company for a
lot longer than I have.' Beth was not sure at all. She had lost
some confidence in her ability over the years.

'You've been there long enough,' Spice said. She'd been
quiet till now, but agreed with Tom's belief that Beth would
be well suited to the job. 'Mr Dalton will choose the person
he thinks is best able to do the job, and the person he thinks
he can work with the best. It has nothing to do with how long
a person has been working there.'

Beth was silent for half a minute. She was thinking it over.

'When's the interview?' Spice asked.

'Next Thursday,' Beth replied.

'Good, that gives us time to practise. We'll start
tomorrow. I'll prepare some questions you might be asked.'

Spice didn't forget. Her determination convinced Beth to
go ahead and apply. The following night, she called Beth to
her room, and they sat together on the bed. 'The interview will
probably begin this way. I'll ask the question, and you answer
it as if I'm Mr Dalton.'

Spice: 'Why do you want this position?'

*Beth: 'I feel my strength is organising things. I like work
that involves detail, and would welcome the opportunity for a
greater challenge. I like to think I'm popular with the other
workers…oops, perhaps I shouldn't say that…and I know
we'd work well together.'*

Spice praised Beth for her answer. 'Rather than say you're popular, which might sound like boasting, it might be better to say that you work well with all the other workers. That will send the same message. And it might be good to say that your children have grown up, giving you more time to show what you're capable of, and to spend more time at work if necessary.'

So, Spice continued to ask questions for the next hour, and to suggest ways to improve Beth's answers.

*

'Margaret Cross and Beth Ellis are going for the job,' Marjorie said with a severe face, 'so that makes three of us.'

'Are you worried Marj?' Wendy asked. 'Do you think the others have a chance?'

'No Wendy, I don't think they have a chance,' Marj answered with a smile. 'You have to agree that I am better than they are. Mr Dalton must know that.'

'And you've been here much longer than they have.' Wendy felt the need to support her friend.

'Yes, and that should count for something. What's more, Margaret can't speak properly. She mumbles. Not what a boss would want in a personal assistant.' Marj was beginning to say nasty things about the other two, her rivals, but not in their earshot. 'And the way she dresses! Aarh! Have you seen her this morning in that purple blouse?'

'What about Beth?' Wendy asked. 'She seems like a nice person, and she seems to get on well with Mr Dalton.'

'Nice? Rubbish! She loves herself. Have you seen the way she walks around the office like Miss La-de-da?'

Marjorie Evers had been with the company for fourteen years. She was a very big, cylinder-shaped top-heavy woman with stick thin legs that she hid by wearing slacks. She had a meaty face that became red and perspired when she was angry. And she was angry a lot of the time. Her loud voice and laugh could be heard around the office.

Wendy Passmore was everything that Marjorie wasn't. She was small and thin where Marj was big. She had a small pale face like a squirrel where Marj's was big and red. She had no confidence at all, and she spoke in a whisper. She often felt the need to apologise even though she'd done nothing wrong.

'You seem very confident about getting the job,' Wendy said.

'Almost certain,' Marj answered with a sly grin. 'I have a few things on my side.'

Wendy was puzzled and didn't answer. So Marj continued. She was obviously pleased with herself, and wanted someone else to know how clever she was.

'I ran off some articles I found on the internet about how not speaking properly and mumbling made people want to get away from you. I sent them to Margaret. She doesn't know it was me. I don't think she will be very confident at the interview.' She smiled. 'I also told her that Mr Dalton liked us to wear very short skirts at interviews.'

'But he hates that!' Wendy cried. 'He's always saying that a woman should be modest and not make a show of herself. He's old-fashioned.'

'That's right,' Marj answered. 'She's going to make a fool of herself,' and her loud laugh could be heard throughout the office.

'And what about Beth?' Wendy asked.

Marj looked particularly pleased. 'You know the report Beth was asked to write for Billson's. It was in an envelope on her desk, all three pages. She just finished it yesterday before she went home. I must say it was very good. I saw her hand it in to Mr Dalton when she arrived this morning. Well, what she doesn't know, is that I stayed back late yesterday, and retyped the report.'

'Why did you do that?' Wendy asked, not understanding Marj's motive.

'You're a bit slow aren't you Wendy. Why do you think? I changed it. I made it so that some sentences don't make sense, and I've made sure that there are at least a dozen spelling mistakes. I don't think Mr Dalton is going to be very impressed.'

'Wow,' was all Wendy could say.

*

There were celebrations at the Ellis home when Beth was given the position of personal assistant to Mr Dalton. He had come into the large office and made the announcement shortly after the interviews. The workers had gathered around Beth's desk to congratulate her.

When she returned home on the Thursday after the interview with the news, Spice had already made a cake. She was confident that Beth would be successful.

'I start on Monday. He asked all the questions we practised,' she told Spice, who didn't seem at all surprised. 'He began with "why do you want this job", and after that, I knew everything was going to be fine. I have you Spice to thank for my success.'

'You got the position Beth,' Spice answered, 'because you were the best person.'

The Ellis family had a special dinner that night. Beth was excited. Tom was delighted. And Scott and Lara were proud of their mother.

'You've looked after us all for years Mum,' Scott said. 'Now it's your turn to do something you really want to do.'

Margaret congratulated Beth the next day at work. 'You deserved it Beth,' she said. 'I realised when Mr Dalton started to ask the questions that I probably wasn't suited for the job. I'm pleased for you.' Beth could see that she really meant it. But she certainly wasn't congratulated by a furious Marj.

She banged things down on her desk, and spoke nastily to everyone who passed by.

'I'm so sorry Marj,' Wendy said, seeing that Marj was annoyed. 'Bad luck.'

'Shut up Wendy,' Marj snapped loudly. 'Luck had nothing to do with it. They haven't heard the last of this.'

Wendy crept back to her desk, wondering what Marj meant. And she was hurt at being spoken to like that. 'They haven't heard the last...' Who were they – Mr. Dalton, Beth, the whole company – and what would 'the last' be. Was Marj thinking of doing something to make people pay for not getting the job?

*

26

Beth enjoyed her new work, and Mr Dalton was pleased and told her so. She liked having a lot of different things to do, and welcomed the responsibility. It was a pleasant change from the sameness of what she'd been doing. In that first week she returned home late each afternoon feeling pleased with herself, and knowing that she was doing well.

The other workers were pleased for her, particularly Margaret with whom she became good friends. Marj was the exception. Even Wendy was pleasant to her as long as Marj wasn't there to see her. Marj wouldn't like that at all.

On the fourth day of her new job, she saw Marj standing in the corridor talking to a new member of staff. She wanted to make peace with Marj even though she had nothing to apologise for. She went over to them, but as soon as she arrived, Marj turned and walked away commenting on how 'it didn't smell very nice around here'.

'Look at her,' Marj told Wendy that lunch time. 'She must think she's the queen, acting so superior.'

Wendy didn't agree, but she didn't dare to say so. Beth didn't behave as if she were superior, and she had always been nice to her.

'Have you ever seen the way Dalton looks at her?' Marj asked Wendy. 'All gooey- eyed. Can't you imagine what it sounds like? Oh Mrs Ellis, would you mind...Oh Beth, it would be great if you could...'

'But isn't he just being nice Marj? He's nice to us all.'

'Even you agreed Wendy that I should have got the job,' Marj said nastily. 'So why do you think I didn't? Don't think too hard now. You might hurt your brain.'

Wendy didn't want to say what she really thought, that Beth would be good at the job, and she was hurt by Marj's insult. She said nothing. So Marj continued.

'It had nothing to do with ability! He gave her the job because he likes her, likes her a lot.'

Marj was suddenly quiet, and Wendy, who had remained silent, could see her thinking, and she could see the light in her eyes. Something big had just occurred to her. Marj was working on a plan.

'What is it?' Wendy asked. 'You're planning something, aren't you?'

'You'll find out soon enough,' Marj answered and walked away. 'There's something important I have to do.'

The next day, she placed a sheet of paper on Wendy's desk, and stood close to Wendy's chair. 'Read this letter,' she demanded. 'Put it flat on the desk. It's important no one sees it. And don't show any surprise.' Wendy read.

Dear Mr Dalton,
I'm so grateful that you gave me the job of your personal assistant. I've admired you so much ever since I started here, but I was a junior worker, and it wasn't my place to tell you so.
Since getting the job, and being able to work so closely with you, my admiration, and dare I say it, my affection for you has grown. I now look forward so much to coming to work each day, so that I can see you.
I hope you don't think I am being too forward in writing this letter, and can only hope that you might feel a little of the way I do. Even if it is only a little, I'll be happy.

Yours,
Beth

Wendy handed the letter back to Marj. 'You're going to give that to Mr Dalton, aren't you? You can't do that,' she said. 'Don't you think that's being cruel. It could hurt them both.'

Marj was annoyed. She'd expected Wendy to be as pleased as she was, and she wanted to hear how well written the letter was. 'Well they both hurt me, didn't they? You don't know what you're talking about Wendy. And if you say one word about this…'

Wendy didn't know how to answer, and was told that the letter would be on Mr Dalton's desk within the hour, and that she'd better not say anything to Beth. Wendy did nothing and would regret it later and apologise to Beth.

Early the following morning, a red-faced Mr Dalton called Beth into his office and closed the door. Beth could see he was looking very serious, and thought it would be about a matter that was to be kept in strict confidence. His concern made her wonder if she had done something wrong.

'I read the letter' he began and looked shy. He waited for Beth to say something.

'What letter was that Mr Dalton?' She had typed several letters the afternoon before.

'I mean, *the* letter. *Your* letter. And please call me Bruce.' He waited again.

Beth didn't know what he was talking about, and didn't know what he expected her to say. She was thinking hard about what letter he might be referring to. Mr Dalton, thinking that Beth might not be saying anything because she was embarrassed at already having said too much, decided to take the lead. She had been daring in writing the letter. It was his turn to say something, or reveal something.

'You said in your letter, you hoped I might feel a little of the way you do. I want you to know that I do. I've liked you the moment you came to work for Dalton and Groves.' His face was red, and he was fidgeting with the folders, pens and stapler on his desk. He was finding it hard to look her in the eyes.

Beth was confused, embarrassed, and felt very uncomfortable. 'Mr Dal... I mean Bruce, do you have this letter I wrote?'

Mr Dalton opened a drawer, took out the letter, and handed it to Beth. She read it, her mouth open in surprise. Mr Dalton could see from her surprise and shock that she hadn't written the letter.

It was awkward for them both. Mr Dalton had admitted to a very strong affection for Beth. He was embarrassed, but it was too late to deny he'd said it. Beth liked her boss, but now that he had admitted to such a strong feeling, she wasn't sure how to rescue him from a sticky situation. It would be unfair to say that what was in the letter was true. It wasn't. But it would be unkind to say she had no feelings for him at all.

He was sitting behind his desk, looking shame-faced. 'I feel I've made a complete ass of myself,' he said. Then he was silent, avoiding her eyes and waiting for her to take the lead.

'Bruce,' she swallowed, 'we both know now that I didn't write the letter. Someone was trying to make trouble for us both. I am fond of you. You've been wonderful to me.' She paused and swallowed again. 'I'm grateful that you told me of your feelings for me, and I'll treasure that...'

'You needn't say any more Beth.' He interrupted, and became silent again.

But Beth couldn't keep quiet. She needed to smooth things over. 'But I do need to. We shouldn't be embarrassed.' She hoped she sounded bright. 'There's nothing wrong with two people saying they're fond of each other. Now, about that package to go to Smithson's.' She tried to return the talk to business matters to save Mr Dalton from his embarrassment.

As she left his office, as white as a sheet and with a sick feeling in her stomach, she wondered if that would be the end of her job, the job she'd only had and enjoyed for a few days. When she passed Marj's desk, she saw her grinning. Wendy looked sad. There were tears in her eyes. There could be no doubt about who had written the letter.

It was a real effort to last through the day. She didn't see Mr Dalton again, but she had plenty of work to do. His office door was closed. He didn't call upon her once, and that was unusual. The hours dragged by before it was time for her to go.

The trip home seemed to take forever. She kept thinking of Marj's grin, Mr Dalton's embarrassment, and her own not very convincing attempts to smooth things over. Tom would be furious, and would be tempted to march into Dalton and Groves tomorrow. She was grateful that Spice would be there to comfort her.

Spice knew as soon as Beth opened the car door that something was very wrong. They sat on the lounge together and Beth cried as she told the story of the day's events.

*

Beth felt great relief the following work day when she wasn't dismissed by Mr Dalton. She knew she had done nothing wrong, but she would have understood if he had decided it was impossible to continue working with her. He was relaxed when he called her to his office and spoke to her, and told her that what she'd said about there being nothing wrong with two people saying they were fond of each other, was true.

'I know you've been worried Beth,' he said, 'but you have done nothing wrong, and it's not going to spoil our working together. It's not going to make things awkward for me, and I hope it won't for you either.'

He also told her that it was clear to him who had written the letter, but he wouldn't rush to do anything. 'She'll just deny it,' he said, 'and then it might become a problem with the law. And I know the report you wrote for Billson's had been changed. You never make a spelling mistake, and certainly not a dozen of them.'

Throughout the day it became apparent that Wendy wasn't spending any time with Marj. Beth saw Marj call Wendy to join her when it was time for morning tea, but Wendy stayed sitting at her desk. She didn't approve of Marj's action in deliberately hurting and embarrassing two people. What satisfaction was there in that? And she felt a little guilty that she had not warned Beth of what Marj was planning to do. Her refusal to go when called did not please Marj at all.

But it didn't stop her teasing Beth at every opportunity that came her way. 'You didn't seem happy the other day,' she said without the hint of a smile. 'I hope it wasn't a broken love affair.' She did not like it that Beth seemed happier now. Perhaps her plan had not worked as well as she'd hoped.

Beth was busy at work in her office space outside Mr Dalton's office, and didn't see Marj go white and start trembling as she listened on the phone, and gave brief, scared answers. If she could have listened, this is what she would have heard:

'Mrs Evers. Am I speaking to Mrs Marjorie Evers at Dalton and Groves?'

'Yes.'

'This is Constable Carolyn Forbes from Strathfield Police Station. You've been reported for a very serious criminal offense, and we have evidence in our possession.'

'What…what…'

'Misrepresentation, Mrs Evers. That means pretending to be someone else to do them harm. Are you understanding me Mrs Evers?'

'Yes…I think so, but if it's only a joke…'

'I think we both know, Mrs Evers, that this was not just a joke. This was a deliberate attempt to cause hurt.'

'But I didn't mean…I just wanted…what might…what will…'

'That is up to the person who made the report, and of course the people you hurt. If they press charges, it will have very serious consequences for you.'

'What…I mean what…'

'Let's not talk about that just yet. We want to hear your story, Mrs Evers, before we continue. We'll expect you at Strathfield police station at 4.00pm. You won't do yourself any favours by being late.'

Marj sat at her desk stunned. Her normally red face was white and there were blotches of purplish-pink on her neck. Her hands were shaking. The office was spared her booming voice. All the workers were at their desks, so who could have made the phone call?

At lunch time, she saw Beth come out of her small office and head towards the kitchen area where most of the workers ate. She hurried towards her.

'Beth, Beth', she said out of breath, 'I've been meaning to congratulate you on getting the position of personal assistant,' and she reached out her hand to shake. 'Did you bring your lunch today. If not, I can get you something at the corner shop. Only take me a minute. Sit down and I'll make you a coffee.'

Beth was confused. It was obvious that Marj wasn't joking. She seemed frightened, but why the change. And what a sudden and dramatic change. She'd been cruel and nasty. Now she couldn't do enough to help and to please.

'I have an urgent letter to type,' she told Marj, 'but I'll have a quick cup of coffee.' She thought it wise to be friends with Marj if friendship and apology was what she was offering. Mr Dalton might be able to explain why Marj was so different. Perhaps he had spoken to her harshly and given her a warning.

She drank her coffee quickly, and listened in disbelief as Marj complimented her on how well she was doing her new job.

She didn't see or hear of Marj for the rest of the afternoon until 3.30 pm. She was speaking to Margaret when they saw Marj quietly leave her desk, take her bag and leave. She obviously didn't want to be seen. Five minutes later she rushed back into the main office. She was crying loudly. 'The tyres, the tyres, all of them.'

All the workers stopped and looked up. Several rushed to help, trying to calm her so they could make sense of what she was saying. 'Whatever is the matter?' they kept asking.

'The tyres. The tyres on my car. All four of them. All flat. Flat,' she howled.

'We'll get help,' someone said.

'In an hour or two you can drive…' another tried to calm her.

'No! No! No! You don't understand. I have to be somewhere at 4.00 pm. It's very important, and I can't be late. I can't! I just can't be!'

'If it's that important, I'll drive you,' someone volunteered.

'No. I don't think so. I…No!' The last thing Marj wanted was for the people at Dalton and Groves to find out she was wanted by the police. That would be the end of her job.

'It sounds hard to believe,' Beth told Spice that night, as she explained the curious happenings at work, 'it may be hard to believe, but I actually felt a little sorry for her.'

'Do you think she's learned her lesson then?' Spice asked.

'Her lesson?' Beth questioned, looking curiously at Spice, and it slowly began to dawn that Spice had something to do with all that had happened. 'Spice.' Her single word was a question.

'Constable Carolyn Forbes from Strathfield Police Station here,' Spice answered, adopting the voice she'd used with Marj. 'Mrs Evers? Marjorie Evers?'

Beth found it hard to believe what she was hearing. 'It was you,' and they both started laughing. They were still laughing with the tears rolling down their faces, when Tom came home and wanted to know what was so funny. He could tell that there had been a happy ending.

'There is a down side,' Spice said to Beth, and she raised a paw to her mouth. 'I'm not sure if I've made a tooth loose chewing holes in those tyres.'

Chapter 3

For the first three months of Spice's stay with the Ellis family, she settled into a routine. She'd get up earlier in the mornings than the rest of the family and get her own breakfast. Sometimes she'd knock gently on Tom and Beth's bedroom door, and ask if they'd like their breakfast in bed. Now that Beth had a more demanding job, she'd often have the family dinner ready when Beth came home.

She couldn't do the heavier outside work, like mowing the lawn or carrying bush rocks to make edges for the gardens. She wasn't tall enough or strong enough, but she was able to weed the gardens very quickly using all four paws, and plant flowers.

Throughout the day, she'd use the home computer to study. Like Donegal, she was particularly interested in how to make life better for refugees, migrants, the homeless and those who had fallen on hard times. To do that, she needed to understand Government rules and regulations. And of course, she was concerned about the welfare of animals. She'd sometimes make phone calls to get important information that wasn't available to most people.

Her night time run was a part of her routine she wouldn't miss. It gave her a chance to be alone with either Beth or Tom. She wasn't as fast as Donegal, but he was super quick. Most of her runs were with Beth, and they'd talk about Scott and Lara, Beth's work, and her own plans as they ran.

She also tried to visit Mrs Rouse at least once a week, and take morning tea. The old woman was very fond of her. They'd have long talks, mainly about what times were like when Mrs Rouse was growing up, what she called 'the good old days', and she was sad when Spice had to go. 'Do you have to go already?' she'd say. 'It seems as if you've only just come. Doesn't time fly? I hope you'll come again soon.'

Spice had become fond of everyone in the family, and had grown to know all the little differences between them. There was Tom's need to have his pencils sharpened, and everything neat and in exactly the same place on his study desk, Scott's need to have other members of the family take an interest and ask him his news rather than have to volunteer it, and Lara's need to be praised for how she looked, how she behaved, and whether boys might find her attractive.

But after a few months of this routine, Spice wondered if there were other important things she could do with her life.

'I feel I should be doing more to help other people,' she told Beth. 'But I'm not sure what.'

Beth suggested some different things she could do, but none of them fired her imagination. 'I'm not one of these people who want to draw attention to themselves,' she answered. 'I think I'm better suited to working "behind the scenes", working without being seen.'

'Take your time Spice,' Beth advised. She resisted asking Spice how old she was. 'Wait till it all becomes clearer.'

*

'I really don't know how he feels Mum,' Lara told Beth, looking a little sad. 'He never tells me. Perhaps he doesn't care.'

'But do you tell him how you feel?' Beth answered.

'Mum!' Lara replied. 'I couldn't do that.'

'Why not? We've always told each other how we feel in this family. You've never had a problem with that.'

'But Mum! He's a boy!'

Lara had a few boyfriends over the years, but nothing serious. They were boys who were friends, and that was all. Most of her dates were in groups of boys and girls. She was nineteen now, and her study and Donegal had taken most of her time.

She met Eric playing competition tennis on a Saturday afternoon. She played against him in the mixed doubles, and it was apparent even then that they liked each other. There was a spark between them. He was a good tennis player, and she felt that he hadn't hit the ball to her as hard as he could have. They saw each other often after that, but their meetings were more accidental than planned. They'd meet at tennis, and at the parties of friends they both knew, and he'd usually drive her home. They'd sit in the car for a long time and talk.

They had been out in groups of six or eight boys and girls, but hadn't been on a date alone. Lara was waiting for him to ask. He was too shy or unsure of himself to do so.

Eric was the only child in his family and was spoiled by his parents. He was tall and thin with a mop of black hair that hung over his forehead. He was a little short-sighted, but that wasn't the reason he didn't always look at Lara while he spoke. While he was the same age as Lara, she was the first girl he'd really liked, and he didn't know what to do about the feeling.

'The next time you see him,' Beth said to Lara, 'you could tell him how you feel about him without making a big thing of it. Just say "I like you Eric" as if it's the most natural thing in the world. It is the most natural thing in the world.'

As luck, or bad luck would have it, Lara saw Eric alone the following day, and they were able to talk. It began with Eric answering Lara's question about what he had done the previous day.

Eric: Last night I was with Mum and Dad. We went to see a film.

Lara: Did you enjoy it? Do you always see a film with your parents?

Eric: Most of the time. I don't go… well, I haven't been with anyone else.

Lara: I'd love to see a film. It's been such a long time.

Silence.

Eric: It was a great film. It was about this man and woman who fell in love, and how they were able to overcome all their problems by talking about them, and considering the other's needs.

Lara: It's really important isn't it, I mean, to be able to talk about things, and to share your feelings with someone you care for?

Eric: Yes, I suppose it is.

Lara: Do you think it's hard for people to talk about how they feel, I mean how they feel about someone?

Eric: I think it's very hard. It must be hard to tell someone how you feel when they might not feel the same way. Imagine how embarrassing that would be.

Lara: But why should it be embarrassing? Even if they don't feel the same way, it shouldn't be embarrassing. Anyway, wouldn't someone have a good idea how the other person feels, from what they say, how they behave, how they look?

Lara was unhappy for the next couple of days. 'I gave him every opportunity Mum, to tell me how he felt. He didn't. I don't think he cares.'

'Did you tell him how you felt?' Beth answered. 'Remember what we discussed before. Eric is just shy. Some boys find it hard to talk about their feelings. It's easier for we girls. My guess is that if you tell him, he'll be able to tell you in return. You need to show him the way.'

'I'll think about it,' Lara replied. 'But I'd really rather he tell me first. Aren't boys supposed to do that?'

'It might have been like that when your dad and I were young. But I don't think that's true anymore,' Beth laughed. 'Girls are taking the lead more and more. I sometimes think girls are the ones who do the asking.'

Spice had been present at both Lara's talks with Beth when she had repeated what had been said between Eric and herself word for word. This is silly, she thought, and decided to do something about it. She waited till she knew Eric would be home, and went to the phone. She practised her best Lara voice for a few seconds and rang.

'It's only me Eric,' she started. Eric sounded pleased. He always looked forward to her ringing. She started to talk immediately of what was worrying Lara. 'Do you remember us talking the other day about it being hard for a lot of people to say what they feel?'

'Yes,' Eric answered. He didn't know what to expect. Lara might be going to ask him how he felt. What would he say? He knew she'd like to know how he felt. Why was it so hard?

'We agreed there was no reason to feel embarrassed about saying you liked someone.' Spice, pretending to be Lara, was preparing the way forward.

'Oh Spice,' the real Lara called from the doorway, not realising Spice was on the phone. Spice, quick as lightning, placed her paw over the mouthpiece, hoping that Eric hadn't heard a second Lara speaking. That would spoil everything!

'Hello. Hello,' she heard Eric at the other end of the line. 'Did you say something? Are you there Lara?'

'I'm here,' Spice said. 'I think we must have been cut off for a second.' She was careful not to say his name. Lara had mouthed 'sorry' and walked away, but Spice didn't want to take the risk of her hearing. How could she possibly explain making a phone call to Eric. Lara would probably never forgive her.

'Where were we, oh yes, we were talking about saying how you feel. Eric, I like you. I like you a lot. I'm not embarrassed to say so.'

There was silence for a few seconds and Spice thought she heard Eric swallow.

'Gee, that's wonderful Lara. I like you too. I like you a lot.'

'I'll go now,' Spice said. 'I just wanted you to know.' She hung up the phone. If Eric had anything further to say, it was better that he does so with the real Lara.

That night, Lara received a phone call from Eric. Beth and Spice were sitting in the family room when the phone rang. 'Lara, there's a really good film at the Odeon. Would you like to go?'

When an excited Lara told them what Eric had said, they both smiled. Beth was pleased, but only one of them knew why there had been a sudden change.

*

'But they did go out together,' Tiffany cried. 'I wouldn't have minded…well, not as much. I don't think I would have anyway, if he'd told me, but he felt he had to keep it a secret.'

Tiffany was sitting in the family room leaning against Spice, telling her why she was so upset. No one else was home. Scott had taken Claire out to a film. She was a girl who worked in the same IT company as he did. It just happened to be the same film and the same night as Lara's date with Eric. Lara didn't approve of what Scott had done, and thought it best to keep it a secret. But Eric, not knowing any better, and not knowing about Tiffany, had mentioned in front of the family how he had seen them.

Tom and Beth really liked Tiffany, and were disappointed. 'Do you think we should say something to Scott?' Tom asked Beth. 'He's free to go out with who he likes, but he should have said something to Tiffany.'

'Yes, he should have,' Beth answered. 'And yet we don't want to be seen as interfering parents. There might be another side to the story. Why don't we wait a while, and see how things work out between them?'

'I hope they work it out,' Tom said. He was holding a photograph he'd taken of Tiffany a month ago. It showed a slim, attractive girl with hazel eyes and long, light brown hair half way down her back, standing in front of a lemon tree in the back yard. 'She's a lovely girl, and she gets on so well with Spice…she loved Donegal too.' Her love of dogs, particularly Donegal and Spice, was a big plus for Tom.

Claire and Scott had been at a meeting of staff at the IT company where they worked. A junior member of staff like themselves, was giving a presentation. He was stuttering and dropping the papers he was reading from. He was making mistakes, and knocked a glass of water off the table. Scott and Claire did not mean to be unkind, but it was so bad it was funny, and they couldn't help smiling and trying not to laugh. As they did so, they looked at each other, and they were suddenly aware of each other, a moment of understanding.

They had seen each other before in the office, but had never really spoken. This was the beginning of their friendship. 'Your turn to speak next week,' she said with a twinkle in her eye, 'do you think it will be as good as that?'

'Nowhere near as good,' Scott answered, and they both laughed.

Claire was a big girl, tall and round, though not fat. She had dark eyes, long dark hair, and caramel coloured skin. Scott would later describe her as 'larger than life', meaning she was so loud, so bright, so 'out there' as Lara would say, that her behaviour didn't seem natural. It seemed exaggerated. She was full of self-confidence.

From the time of that staff meeting, she showed a strong interest in Scott. She made a point of greeting him each day and sitting with him in the lunch room. She brought him small presents on most days - rocklearoad chocolate, Turkish delight, and CD's that she particularly liked for him to borrow.

She wasn't shy like Eric and Lara. Just the opposite. 'I like you Scott,' she told him. 'I think we're well suited to each other. What do you think?' And then she asked him out.

When Tiffany found out about it, she hurried to the Ellis home, and went with Scott to his room to talk. The family knew why and kept out of the way.

'Do you still want to be my boyfriend Scott?' she asked.

'Of course I do,' Scott replied, looking surprised. 'Why do you ask?'

'I heard you took another girl to see a film.' Tiffany wasn't going to play games. She was going to ask him straight out. But it was obvious that she was upset. There were tears in her eyes.

'Why is it such a big deal?' Scott answered almost too quickly, but it was apparent from the colour of his face that he felt ashamed.

'If you'd told me that you were going, I might have understood.' Tiffany was crying now. 'But you kept it a secret. You were never going to tell me. And that makes me think you intend to go out with her again, that you have something to hide.'

'We were just two friends going to a film Tiff.' Scott was also becoming emotional. 'I like Claire, but not as much as I like you.' Tiffany looked at him in surprise when he mentioned 'liking' her. She thought it might be more than just 'liking'.

'If it's that important,' he continued, 'I won't go out with her again.' He reached for Tiffany's hand, and held it, but she did not close her fingers around his.

There was a long silence.

'Then what are you going to tell Claire when she asks you out again? It's obvious that she has set her sights on you.'

'I'm sorry Tiff,' Scott finally said. 'I won't go out with her again. If I'd known…'

Tiffany was grateful for the apology, but wasn't convinced that the matter was over. And she wasn't happy with what Scott had done. They'd never had any disagreement before.

The family knew everything that had happened. They didn't have to hear every word of the discussion to know. Lara was annoyed with Scott, and told him so. Tom and Beth admitted that Scott had made an error of judgment, but wanted to let matters run their course. They hoped and prayed that it would not be the end of Tiffany's relationship with Scott.

Tiffany didn't visit the Ellis home for a few days. She was usually a regular visitor. When she did, her relationship with Scott was cool. They spoke to each other, but their talk was strained. Tiffany spent more time with Spice than with Scott. Matters were made worse when there were a couple of phone calls from Claire when Tiffany was there. Even though Beth answered the phone, and said to Scott, 'it's for you', everyone knew from Scott's brief answers who had called.

For a few days, Scott was like a bear with a sore head. He snapped at Lara when she spoke to him, and had very little to say to Tom and Beth. He tried to talk to Tiffany, and she tried to be tender towards him, but she was hurting too much.

'What can I do?' he asked Spice one night. He knew that Tiffany had been spending a lot of time with her, and that she might have some answers.

She took Scott's hand in her paw, and looked into his eyes. 'You've said you're sorry for not telling her about the film, and I think Tiffany can accept that. She knows you're sorry, but you can't blame her, Scott, for being worried about this Claire girl.'

'But there's nothing…'

'Yes, there is Scott. And there might be a lot more if you let it go on. Tiffany knows, and I think you know that this girl is after you. So, what are you going to do about it?'

'Tell me what to do Spice,' Scott said helplessly.

You know I can use my voice to sound like anyone, whether they're a man or a woman,' Spice said.

'You mean you could ring Claire and talk to her?' Scott was suddenly brighter. 'Could you do that for me Spice? Tell her that I have a girlfriend?'

'I could Scott,' Spice answered. 'But I won't. This is a mess you've got yourself in to, and you need to accept responsibility. You hurt Tiffany, even though you mightn't have intended to, and you can't just walk away from it, and get someone else to clean up the mess. I don't think I need to tell you what you have to do.'

Scott sat still and listened. Neither Tom nor Beth had spoken to him like this. Perhaps they should have. Spice was the voice of reason.

The following day, he found time over lunch to talk to Claire. It wasn't comfortable telling her that his real and only girlfriend was Tiffany, particularly when she'd bought him a box of Turkish delight that very day. Claire was disappointed.

'What will be, will be,' she said, and then she surprised him. 'I knew about your girlfriend, but I didn't know how important she was. I had hopes, of course. But I think I respect you more for being loyal. You're the sort of boyfriend a girl wants.'

'I'm sorry Claire.' He seemed to be doing a lot of apologising lately.

'So am I Scott,' she replied. 'But don't worry. I'm not going to throw a tantrum.'

He phoned Tiffany when he arrived home that night, and told her what he'd done, telling her word for word what had been said. It must have been very convincing, because Tiffany believed every word, and for the first time in many days, he heard tenderness in her voice.

'I'm coming straight over,' she said.

Chapter 4

For several months after Spice's arrival, neither she nor anyone else in the family had faced the question of whether or not Spice's secret talents should be made known to the world. It was finally addressed in a family conference. They all knew that it couldn't be kept a secret forever.

Tom and Scott argued that it would be good to reveal her talents because it was becoming impossible to keep it a secret, particularly when they were talking to others. 'Spice was telling me…' Tom would say to a friend before he realised what he'd said, and laughing, he would quickly change 'Spice' to 'Scott'. Sometimes a person would visit, and there'd be a rush to make sure that Spice wasn't talking to someone, or walking upright around the house or garden.

They also thought that if others knew of Spice's talents, it would make thousands or millions of people around the world think more highly of animals, and particularly dogs. They didn't want to be famous as the owners of Spice. They didn't need to be seen on television or reported in the newspapers. They'd had enough of that with Donegal. They simply wanted dogs to enjoy more respect than some people continued to give them. Respect for dogs would also mean more respect for all animals. And then there was the good that Spice could do when she became known.

'But Tom,' Beth said, 'Spice doesn't want all the attention. She doesn't want to be famous. She wants a quiet life. She might want respect for herself and every other dog, but she doesn't want fame. Lara and Tiffany agreed. 'It would be awful,' Lara added, 'to have all that media attention … people knocking on the door all day and night, people stopping us in the street, and people with cameras hiding behind trees waiting to get a shot of Spice.'

'And there's something else we need to consider,' Tiffany said. 'What happens if Spice suddenly loses her special talents, like Donegal did. There might be a lot of bad publicity that all of it wasn't true, that we'd played a trick of some sort. They might think less of Spice, and lose what respect Spice might win for dogs.'

The family was quiet for a while before Beth turned to Spice. 'What do you think Spice?' she asked. 'It is after all about you.'

'I have been thinking a lot about it,' Spice answered. 'Beth's right about my wanting a quiet life, a life as an important part of this family, but I have to think about more than just me. I have to think about all the dogs of the world, and if my 'coming out' will get them more respect, and affection, and if what I can do saves one dog from being abused, then I don't think I have a choice.' No one disagreed with Spice's reasons.

The next question discussed was how to make Spice's talents known beyond the family. 'A dinner party,' Scott questioned, 'with some important people invited. People who would be believed.' That's what they had done for the 'coming out' of Donegal.

'Possibly,' Tom answered, 'but it might take a while for the news to spread. They would need to have contacts with responsible people in the media. Perhaps we should contact the television stations, and the newspapers, and have a news conference. That way, Spice could reveal her talents 'live', and the news could be spread world-wide over-night.'

'You don't think that might be too sudden, too much too soon,' Beth asked. There was concern in her voice. 'There'll be a media frenzy anyway. What Lara said about reporters hiding in trees will probably happen.' The family was quiet once more. 'Do you have any ideas Spice?' Beth asked.

'Could I show what I can do in front of an audience?' Spice answered. 'Perhaps a big audience, but one that only has a small television coverage. I could sing and walk around the stage with the microphone.'

'The Voice.'

'Australia's Got Talent.' Lara and Scott called out at the same time with great enthusiasm.

Tom and Beth were not sure it was a good idea. 'That doesn't sound like the thing to do Spice if you want a quiet life,' Beth said, but when Lara and Tiffany explained to Spice what happened in the two shows, she thought it might be the best solution, and she chose 'Australia's Got Talent', as the best one to showcase her talents. She didn't want to be coached. She needed to be able to select her own songs, rather than have another person tell her what she had to sing. Her choice was well-timed because auditions had only just been called.

Lara, Tiffany and Scott were excited, and offered to help Spice with what she might do. They knew all the 'hit' songs from national and international singers, and had a lot of advice to give. She could walk around upright, talk, sing, dance, perhaps all of them.

*

'I've put here "Spice the Wonder Dog" for the name of the act, but it says "if under the age of eighteen, list either your parent or legal guardian contact details".' Beth was sitting with Spice filling in the application form for Australia's Got Talent. They both laughed. 'I suppose I should give my name and contact details. I'm supposed to get all the credit for your performance. It also suggests it might be a help if we send a video of what you can do.'

Spice was deep in thought. 'We'll make a video, but not of everything I can do. It has to be a surprise on the night. I'll stand upright for a few seconds and make some high and low sounds that people might think are funny. I won't sing properly on the video, but I'll do just enough to be called in. Of course, I'll do something quite different on the night. It's got to look like any other dog act on the video.'

The application and video were sent, and Beth received a letter asking Spice to appear at the Sydney auditions in a few weeks. Although the family offered to help her rehearse, and Scott and Lara suggested a thousand songs she might sing, Spice wanted to decide on her own act. She was able to watch a few of the televised auditions in other Australian cities, as those in Sydney were held later. This helped her to understand what happened. There was a host who introduced the acts, and four judges who sat facing the stage. When the act was over, three of the judges had to give a 'yes' for the act to go further in the competition. Bad acts could be stopped before they were finished if they were given a red light.

The judges were Jodie, a pop star with many records, waist length brown hair, and who wore tight and very revealing dresses; Natasha, a blond actress with a long history in television soapies who wore shiny silver pants and earrings that brushed her shoulders; Christian, a popular sports identity with little intelligence and no real understanding of any performances except for those in sport; and Simon, the show organiser with links to promotional agencies, and who wore open neck shirts, and always appeared unshaven.

As the time for Spice's appearance approached, the family became more nervous. Apart from excitement, Tom and Beth also became concerned about what might follow with the attention they would get. They needed to be present when it all happened, and were able to buy tickets to be part of the audience. Spice was neither excited nor worried.

Scott and Lara were so nervous, anyone might think they were performing. For Spice it was a means to an end.

On the night, the family and Tiffany sat together close to the stage. They were all anxious. 'Will she be alright?' Beth asked no one in particular. 'She won't get stage-fright, will she?'

They had to sit through seven other acts - a dance group of forty teenagers, an acrobat, a magician who made cards disappear, a man who swallowed a sword, and three singers - before it was Spice's turn. Only three of the acts received enough yes votes from the judges to continue. Two were given a red light, and had to stop and leave the stage. This made the family even more nervous. Tiffany was urging Spice on before she even appeared.

Eventually it was her turn, and she walked onto the stage on all four feet without being announced to the centre of the stage, in front of the microphone that had been fixed on request to one metre in height for when she stood to sing.

'Not another dog act,' Simon complained quietly to Jodie, having turned off his microphone so his comments wouldn't be heard by the television audience. 'Haven't we had enough animal acts. What's this one going to do…jump through hoops, dance…'

'Make a few sounds like words,' Natasha said. 'Look at the microphone.'

'Where's its owner?' Jodie whispered back. 'Perhaps she'll make a big entrance in a moment.'

Natasha and Christian were puzzled, waiting expectantly for the owner or handler to appear on stage. Natasha thought Spice looked very pretty, standing obediently before the microphone and looking at the audience as if she owned the stage. But an act needed more than good looks.

Before they had time to utter another word, and as the audience was hushed, Spice stood upright, took the microphone from its hold, and as the music started softly in the background, she began to sing 'The Bodyguard'. And it wasn't just high and low sounds as it had been in the videotape, or as Natasha had suggested. Her voice was magnificent.

'If I should stay
I would only be in your way'

The judges watched in disbelief, their mouths wide open. Natasha fell off her chair and scrambled to climb up and sit down again, never taking her eyes off Spice. Christian sat perfectly still, gripping the table in front of him. He'd seen some extraordinary things in sports arenas, spectacular goals and tries, come-from-behind wins, but nothing like this. Jodie was shaking her head and mouthing 'no, no, no' over and over again. Simon was watching Spice's mouth as if he doubted it was her singing. Perhaps the sound was coming from somewhere else?

Spice was moving slowly upright across the stage, the microphone in her paws, and making eye contact with everyone in the hall. 'Playing to the audience,' Simon would describe it days later.

'So I'll go but I know
I'll think of you every step of the way'

The audience was deathly quiet. There were no loud 'whoo whoos', or other noises of approval when singers hit high notes. Some people were sitting forward in their seats, wide-eyed, some were rubbing their eyes, and some were crying. 'Pinch me,' a few said to the person next to them. They all knew that they were witnesses to something remarkable.

'And I...will always love you
You
My darling, you'

The family felt very proud. They'd heard Spice practising, but here on such a big stage made the words seem clearer, and the sound richer and purer. She wasn't just a singer. She was a real performer. She knew how to engage an audience like a real professional. With the main melody, Spice's voice became louder and higher, a big sound from such a small body. Then she was quieter again as the second verse began. The audience was living the emotion with her.

'Bittersweet memories
That is all I'm taking with me.'

After the climax of the song, there was a period of silence, stunned silence. There was no immediate applause like thunder. If a pin had dropped, you would have heard it. People had witnessed a miracle and were in awe. Several were still crying. The colour had drained from the faces of others. What do you do after being present at something like that – cheer, or worship in silence?

It took five to ten seconds before a few people began to clap, and almost instantly, the whole audience was on its feet, clapping, cheering and stamping their feet. It only needed someone, or a few to lead the way. The applause continued for a few minutes. Spice remained standing, waiting to hear from the judges. She wasn't bowing, and didn't appear to be excited. She had returned the microphone to its stand.

The judges kept trying to report their opinions on what they'd seen, and each time there was a thunder of applause to stop them. When there was finally enough quiet for them to comment, they were struck dumb. That was a good thing because sections of the audience would not stop calling out and applauding. Natasha had fallen off her chair again, and wasn't able to get up. Jodie wasn't able to speak at all, but raised her hand, mouthing 'yes'. Natasha raised her hand from her lying position on the floor and made a noise that sounded like 'yes'. Christian simply nodded, but was struggling to keep calm, and Simon managed a few words, 'in all my years in this business….,' but couldn't continue. He was thinking of what this meant for the world of entertainment, and what part he could play. He would be regarded as having discovered a talent that defied every law of nature.

The media went wild. The channel that televised Australia's Got Talent made a fortune once the news of Spice's performance spread, and clips of the performance were sought by other channels. It was shown on every television channel in the world. U-Tube viewings climbed into the millions within a few hours.

It was front page news in newspapers throughout the land, with the headlines 'Australia Sure has Got Talent', 'Judges Struck Dumb', 'Whitney Houston Beware', 'Sugar and Spice and Everything Nice', and 'Now We've Seen It All'.

There was controversy too. Even though all the judges had given a 'yes', there was some early opposition from the record companies to giving a $200,000 recording contract to a dog. Their lawyers said there might be problems. They would later regret this early opposition, and realise too late that a record of songs from a singing dog would be a sensation. No one in the live or television audience doubted that Spice was certain to win. The bosses of the channel were furious with the record companies. Future appearances of Spice would be watched by millions, and eventually by billions. Every future appearance on the show would break all ratings records. The channel would be famous across the globe.

Most of the public agreed with the television channel. They were greedy to see more of this remarkable dog. More people would be sitting in front of their televisions than for the Melbourne Cup, the Soccer World Cup final, or the Olympic Games. But it wasn't surprising that there were people who didn't want Spice to continue on the show. They said the performance was brilliant, but thought it wasn't natural. It wasn't how things were meant to be. Some quoted the Bible to support their opinions about the right place of animals in the world.

And Tom and Beth's concerns were realised. As soon as they arrived home, the media knew where Spice lived, and the phone wouldn't stop ringing. It had to be taken from its holder. Reporters and television interviewers knocked on the door day and night. Beth had already decided not to go running after dark with Spice because there would be people with flash cameras hidden behind trees waiting for that single picture that might make them rich. Even as they slept, Tom and Beth could sometimes hear voices, and see the tip of a lit cigarette in the blackness.

Beth thought this might happen. It was the price for being famous. So as soon as they returned home after Spice's performance, she had hidden her with Mrs Rouse who was delighted to have her, and could be trusted to keep a secret. Mrs Rouse had watched the show on television, and didn't even know that Spice could sing. She felt very important, but couldn't share her responsibility with anyone.

Spice wasn't happy with the fame. She knew her performance would set tongues wagging, and would be a surprise for people, but she didn't think the reaction would be this great. She knew she had a sweet voice, but hadn't realised how special it was. Yet it might only have seemed special to the audience because it was coming from a dog. But she still wanted the quiet life she had spoken of earlier.

After a week of dodging the media, Beth decided she would have to get Spice away from the house, so she contacted her friend, Leonie Majors, and asked her to visit wearing a wig of long blond hair, large red-frame glasses, and green corduroy slacks. 'Whatever you wear, make it stand out, and be easy to recognise,' she told Leonie.

Shortly after Leonie had arrived, parked the car outside the garage, and entered the house, Beth switched clothes with her friend, had Tom fetch Spice from next door by hiding her in a wheelie bin, and drove away with Spice in her friend's car. The reporters watching from their hidden spots thought the woman who'd made a brief visit was leaving, and didn't suspect a thing.

Beth had arranged with the family to stay away for a week or two where she couldn't be found until the media attention died down. Once safely hidden, many kilometres away in a remote beach front cottage, she rang the television station and withdrew Spice from Australia's Got Talent. The bosses at the channel were very upset, and after their threats and then their pleadings failed, offered Beth huge sums of money to keep Spice as a contestant. It would be so wonderful for her, they said. Wonderful for your pockets, Beth answered. The viewing public couldn't understand what had happened. Spice and Beth were not interested in continuing on the show. No amount of money was worth the peace and happiness of Spice and her new family, and they all wondered if Spice's 'coming out' had been a good thing after all.

Chapter 5

'How many times do we have to go over it,' Bruno complained.

'We need to agree on every detail,' Vince answered. 'It only takes one little slip-up, and it's all over. Gary, tell us again what you've learned about the Ellis family.'

'You know most of it. It's been written up in every paper in the country. What they don't say is on Tuesday nights, at seven, the parents go to their ballroom dancing, the son leaves at the same time for his touch football, and the daughter stays over with a friend.'

'But the dog's not alone in the house,' Vince said with authority.

'No. The girlfriend, Scott's girlfriend, her name's Tiffany, she stays with the dog.'

'Anything else?' Vince asked.

Gary was becoming annoyed by Vince's questions. 'I've been watching every night now for three weeks. What more do you want to know? How about what they have for breakfast?'

'Yes,' Vince replied, not thinking Gary's question funny at all. 'Every tiny bit of knowledge helps. You never know when and how we might use it.'

'So, tomorrow night we go in,' Vince said. 'Bruno, go over what happens again for us.'

Bruno was a large, dark man with bushy eyebrows, black hair covering his tattooed arms, and a fat face that appeared boneless and cruel like one of the ancient Roman emperors. He began telling the plan Vince called for with a heavy accent.

'I drive the van up the driveway, no headlights, and slow so it can't be heard. I stop as close as I can to the garage door. Before I do, I stick the sign on the van saying TCN news. You and Gary follow close behind the van so it shields you from anyone looking out the house windows. Gary goes around the back to see if there are any open doors or windows. He carries a camera on a tripod, in case someone is looking at us through binoculars.'

Gary, thin, sandy-haired, with a pock marked face and a long neck but no chin, making him look like an ostrich, nodded.

'You,' Bruno looked at Vince, 'go to the front door, and be ready to say you're a reporter. The girl probably won't answer, because she'll have been told not to, and if she doesn't, and all the doors and windows are locked, Gary uses the brick, wrapped in a towel to smash the glass around the back.'

Vince, more respectable looking than the others, always dressed in a pressed pale blue shirt and tie, continued. 'We need to be out in thirty seconds. There may be alarms, and we might not even hear them. They might sound in a police station somewhere. Gary, you tie up and gag the girl. Don't hurt her unless you have to. She's not big, so she shouldn't put up much of a fight. Make very sure she doesn't scream or we'll have the media world charging in. Bruno, you grab the dog and put it in the van. Make sure you wear gloves and put some chloroform on the towel, so the dog won't fight. You don't want a nasty bite to get infected.'

'I checked the hide-away yesterday,' Gary added. 'It's been deserted for years, no one around, and hidden in the middle of the bush. There's a room to lock the dog in. The drive took exactly one hour and fifty-seven minutes from here.'

'Good man,' Vince praised him. 'That's the kind of detail that's important. It's all going to work out well.'

'But Vince,' Bruno wanted a final word. 'We're only asking for a million dollars! This dog can talk, sing, read, and lots more. People all over the world would like to get hold of her. We could ask twenty times that.'

Vince frowned. He knew what they were doing would cause a sensation. The more money they asked for, the greater the risk. They would be pursued to the ends of the earth, and not just by police in their own country. If anything did go wrong, it might be better that they hadn't asked for too much. The bigger the ransom, the bigger the crime. Bruno and Gary were waiting for his reply. How did they think people in other countries would know who had the dog, how would they be able to contact interested parties, and how could they get it out of the country? 'We'll have time to think about that,' he said.

*

It was two months since Beth had returned home with Spice from their beach-front hideaway. They had been away for ten days, and in that time, Tom had spoken to the newspapers and appeared on television, asking the public to respect their privacy. Most of them did. He had arranged for their phone number to be answered by a secretary at another location, and it was no surprise that even after Tom's request, she was answering the phone calls all day. They came from all over the country and from overseas, wanting Spice to sing at special events like the grand finals of sporting events and Royal Command performances, and in front of Presidents, Kings and Queens.

There was even an occasional call asking Spice to sing at the wedding of some old school friends of Scott and Lara. 'Remember me Lara, Emily Morton from 4A at Dural Primary School,' the caller might begin. 'It's a big ask I know, but I was wondering if…'

While Tom wanted to hire a security man to watch the house day and night, Beth and Spice didn't think it was necessary. 'It's just someone else to be watching what we're doing,' Beth said, 'and the media camped out there,' she pointed to the field across the road, 'is our security.'

So, on a Tuesday night, Tom and Beth departed for their weekly ballroom dancing. Beth was carefree and looking forward to showing off a particular dance step she'd been practising. But Tom, even after two months, was a little anxious. 'We're only a phone call away,' he said to Tiffany. 'You have my mobile number.'

Tiffany didn't see or hear the van crawl quietly down the drive. She did hear the knock at the front door. 'He looks respectable enough,' Spice said to Tiffany, as they both watched behind a curtain in the upstairs window. 'He's wearing a suit and tie.' But they were both under strict instructions not to answer or let anyone in the house.

Spice, with a dog's acute hearing, heard the noise downstairs and warned Tiffany. But it was too late. Vince's knocking at the front door had been a diversion. It had captured their interest. Gary, who'd been able to force a downstairs window without breaking the glass, grabbed Tiffany from behind, putting his hand over her mouth, and signing to her with the other hand to stay quiet as he pushed a handkerchief into her mouth, and having pushed her down on the family room floor, he tied her arms and legs. He'd knotted the rope in loops before he entered the house so he only had to slip it over Tiffany's wrists and ankles. That would make the task as quick as possible.

Bruno was even rougher with Spice. He lifted her off the floor by a front leg, held her against his body with a muscled and tattooed arm, and rubbed the chloroform rag in her face. Spice struggled but Bruno was too strong.

As Vince had planned, they were outside in less than thirty seconds. Spice was bundled into the van. No alarm had sounded in the house, but they knew one was probably alerting the police somewhere else. Tiffany was tied in such a way that she couldn't move.

Bruno drove for a while without lights, then continued slowly along back streets so he wouldn't alert the police. There was very little traffic on the roads. Vince sat next to Bruno, and Gary sat in the back with a firm hand on Spice. He still held the rag in case she put up a struggle.

All she could see from her position lying on the back seat was the black of night and a feast of stars in the sky. She felt woozy from the chloroform, and the swaying of the van, and it didn't help that she couldn't sit upright. She tried to determine the route the van was taking. That information might be helpful later. The men said nothing.

'Where are you taking me?' Spice finally asked, feeling a little ill. There was no answer. 'What do you want with me?' she asked again. But Vince had told Gary and Bruno not to talk in front of her. 'Remember, she can imitate voices,' he'd told them. 'If we were ever suspected, the police could identify us from her imitating our voices.'

They must have driven for a couple of hours, before the van made a sharp turn, and travelled along what Spice reckoned must have been a rough dirt road. Bruno was driving slowly and swerving, obviously trying to avoid pot holes. Branches sometimes brushed against the sides of the van. She could see the tops of trees on all sides, and hear the noise from cicadas. There was no moon. Her leg was hurting where Bruno had grabbed her, and held her dangling by it.

When they arrived at their destination, she was lifted from the back seat, carried inside, and locked in a small room which might have been the pantry. It had no windows and was bare except for shelves around the walls that once might have stored food. There was no food there now. And there was no mattress or rug. Just bare boards.

She made sure she had a good look at the house in case she had to recognise it later. It was an old wooden shack in the middle of the bush. Sheets of tin had worked loose from the roof and threatened to fall. The paint was peeling from the wooden walls in large flakes. The front veranda of wooden planks had collapsed in several places, and the bush had advanced, hugging the walls. It smelled like mould inside. A large lizard escaped as they entered. No one could have lived there for a long time.

She could hear the hushed voices of the men, though she couldn't make out what they were saying. They were all talking quickly, probably excited, knowing that the first part of their plan had gone well. One of them laughed. He started to talk loudly and was shushed by another. She walked around her small prison, but there was no escaping, so she lay down to wait.

*

In the Ellis house, Tiffany was very upset, and blamed herself. 'It's all my fault,' she kept saying to Beth. 'I should have kept a closer watch. What will they do with poor Spice?'

Beth and Tom had come home to find Tiffany on the family room floor. She had been able to get herself into a sitting position, but could do no more. She felt as if she were choking on the handkerchief that had been shoved into her mouth. They didn't need to be told what had happened. Scott returned a few minutes later and comforted her. He was furious. 'Just wait till I get my hands on them,' he warned.

'It is not your fault,' both Beth and Tom told her. 'There was nothing, nothing you could have done.' They both felt guilty. They hadn't hired a security man to watch the house, and Tiffany was left to be the one to face the threat alone. They were really the ones to blame. What if Tiffany had been injured, or even worse? Even now, she had bruises on her arms, and the rope had bitten her wrists and ankles.

The police were called, and Detective Sellers, an officer who'd had experience investigating kidnapping was put in charge. He called the family together, Tom, Beth, Scott, Lara and Tiffany, and told them that it was important that Spice's kidnapping be kept a secret. If there was to be any chance of Spice's safe return, it must be kept from the media. If it became known, people everywhere in the state would be looking, and hoping to become famous with her capture. That would be a great danger to Spice's life.

'I've told them up there,' he pointed to where the media were camped, 'that I've come to ask Spice to sing at the Police Charity Ball.'

'Then what can you do?' Lara asked impatiently.

'Wait,' Detective Sellers replied. 'They will contact you soon, perhaps in a day or two, and demand a ransom. When we know what they want, we will have an idea what to do. I'll have an officer here all day and night to listen in to your phone calls. I know it's hard, but there's nothing more we can do. I'd like to stay here myself if that is alright by you.'

It was already the early hours of the morning, and the family took it in turns to stay up in case the phone rang. Beth sat up with Scott and Tiffany. Tom sat up with Lara. But none of them was able to sleep. The phone didn't ring.

Time seemed to drag. Every minute was like an hour. The next day Sellers and the constable were served breakfast and lunch. Tom and Beth were concerned that the kidnappers might kill Spice without even asking for money. She might be dead already. Or they might wait to get the money and then kill her. 'They'll call,' Sellers told them, and they did.

It was late afternoon when the phone rang. The family ran to the phone and Tom was selected to answer. The constable was listening and signalled to Tom after a few rings when he could answer. He was listening to, and recording the call.

'We've got your dog,' the caller said. His voice sounded strange as if he'd covered the mouthpiece of the phone with something. He was speaking quickly. 'It'll cost you three million to get her back.' Vince had obviously changed his mind about the ransom and tripled the price. 'Get the money. We'll be in touch about how to deliver it. If you contact the police, you'll never see your precious…' The phone crackled and went dead. Tom didn't get a chance to ask the caller to let Spice speak to him as proof that she was still alive.

'Anything?' Sellers asked, hoping that there might have been time to trace the call. The constable shook his head.

'I'm afraid all we can do is wait,' Sellers said. This is how they all operate. The first call is to tell you they have the victim, and to name a price so you have time to get the money. The second call tells you how to get the money to them. You have to be patient. They mightn't call for two or three days.'

'Why?' Tiffany asked.

'They want you out of your mind with tiredness. They want to make sure you haven't told anyone. That's why it's important one of their buddies doesn't see me coming and going, and let them know. They probably have someone watching. And they want you desperate, so you're more likely to give them what they want.'

*

When the first call was made, Spice had been in the small, dark room for nearly twenty-four hours. She could see in the dark, but there was nothing to look at except the warped and empty shelves around the three walls and spider web hanging from a corner of the ceiling. There was no handle on the door, so she couldn't let herself out and steal away. She'd been given no food at all, and only once had the door been opened when Vince, with his face hidden in a balaclava, bought her a bowl of water. She felt weak and ached all over. The floor was rough wood.

The only sounds that made their way into the room were the voices of the men, but even with a dog's hearing, Spice could only make out snatches of what they were saying. She heard, 'give them time,' 'let them stew,' and 'three million.' She knew she'd been kidnapped, she knew she was being held for a ransom, and she knew that sometimes, when things weren't going well, kidnappers panicked and killed the victim to cover their tracks.

She knew that Beth and Tom would be doing everything they could to find and free her, but that her fate was to some extent in her own hands, or paws, and that she was going to have to use her wits. She was also worried that Tiffany might have been hurt.

Another day dragged by. Vince opened the door, but only enough to fetch and refill her water bowl, and throw in one sugar-coated biscuit. He watched as Spice ate the biscuit with a single bite, and lapped up the water. He obviously had no idea of a dog's eating needs.

That night when Vince checked on her again, he found her lying still on the floor, panting rapidly and making terrible rasping noises in her throat. He gave her a gentle kick but it made no difference.

'Bruno, Gary, get in here,' he called, forgetting the need to keep silent, and the two men hurried to join him at the door, hiding their faces as they came. Vince was frowning.

'Hell,' he said. 'Everything was going so well.'

'It still is,' Bruno replied, not seeing any problem.

'She's sick,' Vince answered. 'Look at her.'

'So what?' Gary said, and gave Spice a fierce kick. 'Are you sure she's sick and not just pretending.' Spice gave a quiet groan when she was kicked, and not the yelp that might have been expected if she was well. She rolled onto her side, and her panting became even faster. The strangled noises in her throat alarmed them all.

'We don't need her,' Bruno added. 'Let her die here, while we go and collect the three mills.'

Gary was nodding. 'You're getting soft in your old age Vince,' he said.

'Soft, nothing,' Vince replied feeling insulted. 'Think, you two idiots. No one's going to give us a cent, if they don't see the dog is alright. This dog is our meal ticket!'

'But we can insist on getting the money first,' Gary said, though he was starting to have doubts.

'We need the dog to be in reasonable condition when we swap the dog for the money,' Vince insisted. 'It's a very special dog,' he said. 'Think what it means to scientists all over the world. People will want to see the dog before they hand over the money.'

'You're not suggesting that we take the dog to a vet, are you?' Bruno asked. 'People might not have heard that we've kidnapped her, but they'll certainly recognise her.'

The three men were silent for a minute, and as they were thinking, Spice's breathing continued rapidly and became softer. Foam appeared around her mouth.

'We'd better hurry,' Vince said. 'She looks to be slipping away. We need to find a way of disguising her.'

'We could use dye to change her colour, or shave off some fur,' Gary contributed. 'Perhaps both.'

So, while Vince investigated where they could find the nearest vet, Gary and Bruno worked on Spice's disguise. Gary used scissors to shorten the hair hanging from her sides, and removed some of the hair from around her ears. Bruno darkened her snout, but was careful not to make the changes too obvious. A vet would not be easily fooled. You couldn't risk dye coming off on the vet's fingers.

'Good job,' Vince praised the effort, shutting the lid of his iPad. 'There's a vet about thirty kilometres away. Here's how we'll do it. You two are my brothers. You'll sit in the waiting room showing concern. Shut up and let me do the talking.'

'Boo hoo,' Gary interrupted, trying to be funny.

'I'll insist I'm with the vet when the dog is being examined,' Vince continued. 'We can't risk her talking to the vet. I'll try and get some medicine and be out with the dog as soon as possible. Whatever happens, we can't leave her there.'

'But what if she does talk to the vet?' Bruno asked. 'You can't stop her.'

'She won't while I'm there,' Vince answered, 'because she'll know it would mean the end for the vet, and for her. She won't risk it.'

'What if she needs more than just medicine?' Gary asked.

'We'll cross that bridge when we come to it,' Vince answered.

Vince carried Spice to the van, and sat in the back with her while Gary took his place in the front. A slice of moon was already high in the sky. The van bumped along the rocky road through the trees until it came to a smooth road. 'Take the next left,' Spice heard Vince say after they'd been driving for twenty minutes.

'Vince?' There was a question in Gary's voice. 'It's night. The place might be closed.'

'I wondered about that too,' Vince replied. 'But there should be someone there to look after the sick animals. Fingers crossed.'

The vet's place, a long single-story building set well back from the road, was in darkness when they arrived.

'Doesn't look good,' Bruno said. 'Why don't we just leave the dog here, and have a go at getting the money. We planned on keeping our faces hidden from the dog, and now she's seen us all.'

'And she's heard our voices too,' Gary added. He was on Bruno's side.

But Vince wasn't going to give up so easily. 'Watch the dog,' he said to Gary, and marched up to the front door and knocked. There was no answer. But after his second knock, a light came on, and a young woman in a dressing gown opened the door.

'I'm very sorry,' Vince said in his best voice, 'I know it's late but my brothers and I have a very sick dog. She means the world to us, and we're all really upset. If we leave it till the morning, it might be too late.' He looked at Gary and Bruno standing behind him, and they played their part by nodding. 'Would it be at all possible to see the vet?'

'I'm Christie Danvers,' the tall woman with fair skin, short brown hair and green eyes replied. 'I am the vet. You'd better bring the dog in.' She sounded weary as if she'd been wakened from sleep, and waited for Vince to fetch Spice from the van and carry her into the examination room. Her panting had stopped.

'Would you mind if I stayed while you examined her?' Vince asked in his sweetest voice. 'She gets quite upset if I'm not around when things aren't going well.' He put his hand in his pocket where there might have been a knife or a gun. It could have been a warning for Spice.

'Not a problem,' Christie answered. 'Most of the owners want to be nearby to comfort their pets.'

So, Vince carried Spice to a high padded table in the examination room. It was bare except for a bench and cupboards that stored surgical instruments. There was no window.

As soon as Christie began to examine Spice, starting by feeling around her neck, Spice began to make loud dog noises. Christie didn't seem to be worried. Vince was. If she could make such loud dog noises, she might start talking like a person. And if she were really sick, how could she make such a loud noise.

'Why all the noise?' he asked nervously, as Spice continued. 'Is she in pain?'

'No.' Christie laughed. 'She's trying to communicate with other dogs. Can't you tell when a dog is talking?'

Lady, Vince thought to himself, and smiled, feeling relief. If only you knew how this dog could talk…. and sing.

Christie had run her hands over Spice's whole body, and had looked in her mouth, ears and eyes. She seemed to be taking a long time with her examination. 'I don't think there's anything very wrong with her,' she said. 'I think I should keep her here for the night, and keep an eye on her. If she's alright, I can phone you, and you could collect her in the morning.'

'That won't be necessary,' Vince answered, thinking that Spice might have been fooling him, and trying to hide his anger. He grabbed hold of her from the examination table, but before he could lift her and carry her to the van, there was a terrible noise of barking, and two dogs, a boxer and a Doberman, charged into the room and knocked him to the ground so that he lost his grip on Spice.

As he lay on the floor, not daring to move, with the two dogs standing over him and snarling, their teeth bared, he heard Bruno curse and Gary yell as they were attacked by three cats with very sharp claws. A parrot screeched and stood on Bruno's head, trying to peck his eyes. There was a loud crash as a horse knocked the front door off its hinges, charged into the room, and kicked Gary in the stomach.

Even with the deafening barking, meowing, neighing, screeching, and yells of the wounded, Christie managed to ring the police. She hadn't been fooled. As a lover of dogs, she had recognised Spice instantly, and allowed the animals, some of them her patients and some her pets, to stand guard until the police arrived. 'Did they really think I'd be fooled by black dye on her snout?' she later told the police.

The three men were handcuffed and taken away, and the police, on hearing from Christie that the dog was Spice, returned her to the Ellis home where she was hugged, stroked and fed by her grateful and tearful family. Sellers was satisfied and relieved that nothing terrible had happened to Spice while he was in charge. That would not have looked good on his record.

'It takes something like this,' Beth told Spice with tears in her eyes, 'to make me realise how important someone is. It would have been terrible if something had happened to you.'

'And it takes something like this,' Spice replied, 'to make me realise how important you and your whole family are. I felt very alone.'

Tiffany cuddled Spice for a long while, and kept telling her that she was sorry, and that she was to blame for her capture. 'I'm the one who should be sorry,' Spice told her. 'I should have heard them coming.'

It didn't take long for the media to learn what had happened. It was reported on all television stations in Australia, and the newspapers carried the headlines 'Animals Defeat Dognapping', 'Spice Outwits her Captors', and 'Dog Gone'. Even more reporters could be seen hiding near the Ellis house to catch a photo of the even more famous dog. Beth wondered if she was going to have to take Spice away again to escape the attention.

Christie's veterinary practice, a small out-of-the-way practice in a country area, became so popular with people wanting to take their sick animals to where Spice had been, she had to take on new staff and build more rooms to cope with the demand.

Chapter 6

It was a month since Spice had been rescued from her kidnappers. The family had weathered the frantic media attention, though the requests for Spice to sing or talk at various important meetings or weddings kept coming. She didn't have to pretend now that she was sick. She really was.

Beth was the first to notice. She'd never known a time when Spice didn't want to go on their evening walk or run. It was one activity they both looked forward to so much. It was their time alone. 'I'm just so tired,' Spice told Beth. 'I don't seem to have any strength.' Beth was concerned, but thought the tiredness might pass. 'I get tired too,' she told Spice. 'The years are creeping up on us.'

It became obvious to the other members of the family when Spice didn't or couldn't eat. She sat at the table with them, but while she played with the food on her spoon, none of it found its way to her mouth.

Tiffany, a frequent visitor to the house, was anxious and asked her what she was feeling. All Spice said was that she wasn't feeling very full of life. It wasn't that she didn't want to answer all the questions of concern that Tiffany fired at her. She didn't know what the matter was.

A day or two later, the family had real cause for alarm. It wasn't even after the breakfast Spice couldn't eat that she began to vomit. And not long after that, she had serious diarrhea. 'I'm so sorry,' she said to the family with a faint scratchy voice. 'I feel so embarrassed.'

'Don't be embarrassed Spice,' Lara told her. 'We've all been sick like that. It's food poisoning. You've eaten something that didn't agree with you.'

'I'm worried Tom,' Beth said. 'It might go away, but it could be a lot more serious. I think it's time we took Spice to a vet. What do you think Spice?' But Spice was being sick again, and couldn't answer.

'Christie Danvers?' Tom asked.

'It's a two-hour drive,' Beth answered. 'This is urgent. We'd better settle for the vet in Galston.'

Tom and Beth helped Spice to the car, placed cushions for her on the back seat, and drove the few kilometres to the vet. She was sick on the way.

An elderly Mr Spade who'd been the only vet in Galston for thirty years examined Spice immediately. He didn't recognise the famous dog, either because sickness had changed her appearance, or because he wasn't a television watcher. He gave the impression of being more interested in books than popular culture. He had Tom lift Spice onto the examination table. It was similar to the one she'd been placed on at Christie Danvers' place.

He began the examination, asking Tom and Beth several questions, and nodding after they answered each one. 'I'd like to run a blood test,' he told them.

'Of course,' Beth replied. 'But do you have any idea of what the problem might be?'

Mr Spade usually didn't like to answer this question until he was certain, but he could see that Beth really wanted to know.

'I'm almost certain,' he began, 'of course I could be wrong, but I think it's Parvovirus. You've told me she has all the symptoms, lethargy or not wanting to do anything, vomiting, diarrhea, and I can tell that she has already lost some weight and has a fever.'

Beth and Tom were now really worried. 'Tell us about this, what is it, Parvo…' Beth asked, feeling a little sick from worry herself.

'Parvovirus is a virus,' Mr Spade began, 'that affects the body's ability to absorb nutrients or the good things in food, so the dog becomes weak from not having enough protein and liquid.'

'But where did this virus come from, and how dangerous is it?' Beth wanted to know everything about it.

'It comes from contact with another infected dog, or from the pooh of an infected dog.'

'But Spice wouldn't have…' Tom replied, but then thought of the brief time she'd spent with the kidnappers. Perhaps it was one of the dogs at Christie's place, one of the dogs that saved her from harm. There were a few seconds of silence.

'In answer to the second part of your question,' Mr Spade continued, 'there's a seventy percent survival rate.' He saw the look on Beth's face, and knew that if he'd said ninety-five percent, it still would have distressed her. He believed in telling his clients the truth, even if it did hurt.

'So, what happens now?' Tom asked. Beth was looking tenderly at Spice, and Spice was looking back as if to say 'don't worry.'

'Well she can't go home,' Mr Spade said, trying to sound comforting. 'She might be here for some time. All we can do if it is parvovirus is to treat the symptoms. We'll put her on an intravenous drip to keep up the fluids she's lost from her diarrhea. And there are a variety of drugs we can use to stop the vomiting, and fight any parasites.'

Tom and Beth left feeling very depressed. 'Did you see where they were going to keep her?' Beth said to Tom. They'd been shown a small room with no windows and a bed that was more a bench than a bed. And they'd been told that she couldn't be put with other animals because parvovirus was very contagious. 'We can't let her stay there. We just can't,' and she began to cry.

When they returned home, Beth rang the nearest hospital, never thinking at the time that they would not take a dog. 'But she's almost human,' she told the hospital administrator. 'You've seen her talking and singing on the television.' For once she thought there might be some benefits from the media attention.

'I'm sorry madam,' was the answer. 'There are very strict rules about animals in hospitals. As much as I might like to…'

After receiving the same answer at two other hospitals, she managed to contact the local member of parliament, and being a lover of dogs, he contacted the Minister for Health. 'Are you out of your mind,' the answer came back from the Minister who wasn't fond of dogs. 'Wait a minute,' he said sarcastically, 'I'll see if the hospital has a spare bed for my kid's pet tortoise, budgerigar and guinea pig,' and hung up.

Beth then rang Christie Danvers and learned that the builders had already finished a new wing to her animal hospital, and Christie described how clean and modern it was. She would be delighted to have Spice as her first patient. She felt she owed the Ellis family her sudden good fortune. So even though it meant a two-hour drive, Spice was placed with Christie. The results of the blood tests confirmed that Spice did have parvovirus.

The family decided they would each take turns in visiting. Scott now had his own second-hand car, and Christie told Beth she was welcome to stay the night with her whenever she liked. She did.

For the next couple of weeks, at least one of the family sat with Spice for most of the day, and Christie was very attentive. The vomiting and diarrhea continued for some time, Spice had already lost a lot of weight, and was skin and bones.

'She looks so ill,' Beth said to Christie. 'What's wrong with her mouth and eyes?'

'It happens with parvovirus,' Christie explained. 'The wet tissue of the eyes and mouth becomes red, and you've probably noticed that her heart is beating faster. I'm doing all I can Beth,' and she placed her hand on Beth's shoulder.

It was hard, particularly for the first few days, seeing Spice on a drip and seeming to be asleep, but after that she began to recover slowly and was able to talk. Beth was there most of the time. Tiffany was a frequent visitor, and while Spice was still weak, she'd read to her. She liked *Lassie, Rin Tin Tin, and Black Beauty*. Lara would brush her fur every time she visited. Tom would tell her stories about his fondest and funniest memories of Donegal, but had to be careful that she didn't laugh too much and hurt her chest. Scott would tease her by asking her to sing, and would start singing himself. That also made her laugh because Scott couldn't hold a tune.

She did eventually get better. 'She can go home,' Christie told Beth. It was a day Beth had been waiting for impatiently.

'I wish I could keep her,' and she laughed. 'I don't often get a patient who thanks me every time I do something for them.'

'Completely cured then,' a relieved Beth said. It was more a question than a statement.

'It *is* a virus,' Christie answered, 'so it will always be in her system, but she'll be alright now. She still needs plenty of rest. She'll be weak for a while. A gentle walk is alright, but not too far.'

The family was excited and prepared a small celebration when she returned home. There was no rich food because they knew her body was not yet ready to cope with it. Tiffany had bought 'welcome home' balloons.

It was fortunate that Spice returned when she did, because the following day Beth received a shock. She learned that her good friend Leonie Gregson was seriously ill in hospital. Spice knew Leonie, and she knew of her fondness for Donegal.

'I want to see her,' she told Beth.

Beth looked surprised. 'I don't think she's well enough,' she answered. 'And I don't think you are either.'

'Beth,' Spice looked at her with pleading eyes. 'I really want to see her. I learned a lot about myself when I was sick. And I learned a lot about what people must experience…all the dark thoughts they must have, the mixed-up feelings they can't tell anyone, all the ways they must think back over their life…things they'd done or should have done.'

Beth could see how important it was for Spice. She had learned the hard way that animals could not be admitted to hospital as patients, but she had also heard that dogs were sometimes allowed to visit hospitals, as long as they were obedient, sweet-tempered, and wouldn't jump up on the patient. They had to be under strict supervision. It was widely believed that a visit from a dog brought a lot of pleasure to children and to old people in particular.

The hospital in which Leonie was a patient agreed to the visit, but insisted that Spice be accompanied by a nurse. Some patients were allowed to pat the dog, they were told, but the dog could not lick them. At least the hospital didn't insist on Spice being on a leash.

Beth drove Spice to the hospital and spent some time with Leonie by herself, before she returned to the waiting room for the nurse to take Spice from Tiffany.

'Don't expect too much Spice,' Beth warned her. 'She's very depressed.'

The nurse, a young Australian-Chinese woman sat by the door as Spice sat by the bed of a delighted Leonie. They spoke quietly together. Leonie could often be seen patting Spice. And Spice rested her paw on Leonie's arm. They seemed to be engaged in a conversation that was full of meaning.

The nurse allowed the meeting to go for longer than the time normally allowed. She was amazed to see an animal and a person talking so intently together. It looked as if they were sharing something very deep.

Before returning Spice to Beth, the nurse took her around various wards of the hospital. Spice hadn't been 'cleared' to meet other patients, but she was able to see the patients in their beds, some of them looking frail and in pain. Sometimes there were six to a room with curtains drawn around the beds. Some of them saw her as she passed their room, and their faces lit up with pleasure. She felt sad. Most of the humans she'd known didn't get sick. But she realised they were just as likely to be sick as animals. Probably more so.

Months later, when Leonie had finally recovered, she would tell Beth how important, and how comforting that meeting with Spice had been. 'It really cheered me,' she said. 'More than that…she made me see things differently. She was so sensitive to my feelings.'

At dinner, the night after her visit to Leonie, she told the family that she would like to continue to visit hospitals. She'd heard mention of palliative care wards, places where patients were so sick they were likely to die. She told them she'd like to visit those wards.

'Won't that upset you?' Tom asked. Beth and Lara nodded their agreement. 'They might not be very happy places.'

After a few seconds of thought, Spice answered. 'I can feel for those people, and I can feel with them. I might be able to make them happy, or give them a little comfort as their life draws to a close. I know you all care, but I think I have to try.'

So it was arranged, and because the patients were in palliative care wards where they were seriously ill, and there wasn't much more that could be done for them, except to make them comfortable, the hospitals were glad to have Spice visit.

Her first patient was Mavis Crowley, who didn't seem all that surprised by having a visit from a walking and talking dog, even though she wasn't aware of the media reports. 'Nothing much surprises me dear. Ninety-six,' she said, as though her age explained her lack of surprise, and then as if she could anticipate the first question Spice might ask, 'things are just failing in this old body, giving up on me.'

Spice knew there was a time to talk and a time to listen. This was a time to listen.

'I've had a good life,' Mavis began. 'Reg was wonderful, bless him. I was so lucky to have had such a man. Treated me like a princess he did. Your wish is my command he used to say, and he meant it. I'll always be there for you he said, but he wasn't. No fault of his though poor man. He was taken from me in France in the war over seventy years ago. But I have no regrets. It's better to have loved and lost than never to have loved at all, or so they say.'

She stopped for a while and held Spice's arm in her bent fingers, as if it was the most natural thing to do. 'I had a dog, a little poodle called Bliss. We'd talk to each other all day. I seem to remember doing most of the talking.' She scratched her head. 'I don't think she talked much at all.'

'Do you have many visitors?' Spice asked.

'Oh yes,' Mavis answered with pleasure. 'I'm very fortunate. The nurses are always coming in, bless them. They're so lovely. Amity, Michelle, and Ruth's a real scream. Makes me laugh. I never had children. We both wanted them so much, but we decided to wait till Reg got back from the war. I've had a good life. Ninety-three. Things are just failing…Reg was wonderful bless him. Treated me like a princess. I was so lucky…'

Spice listened for another fifteen minutes until Mavis began to get tired. She asked the occasional question to help her through the brief story of her life. Sometimes Mavis would stop, and Spice had to remind her what she'd just been saying. It was a story Mavis needed to tell.

When Spice announced that she was going, Mavis reached out to her, her painfully thin body like a skeleton draped with skin emerging from beneath the sheets. 'This has been a very happy day,' she said with emotion. 'I enjoyed our talk. I'm so glad I've met you dear. I know you're busy but it would be wonderful to see you again. It makes me feel the world is heading in the right direction.'

Her second patient, Tony Gianoppolous was in the palliative care ward of another hospital. Unlike Mavis, he would have sudden fits of pain, but was able to increase the amount of morphine in the drip attached to his arm.

He was surprised by seeing Spice. 'Tina told me all about you. I wish she were here now. Wait till I tell her.'

Spice had been advised not to ask him about his sickness. She was still learning how to treat the patients, and started by asking him about Tina and his family.

'My parents came out to Australia from Greece in the 1980s,' he answered. 'They have a little farm now in Arcadia, vegetables and hens, eggs. That's what they had back home. They come to see me most days. Tina's my girlfriend. She's Italian. She was here earlier. We were going to be married. It's alright Spice, I say "were" because I know I'm not getting out of here. I get annoyed by people, my family mostly, trying to pretend otherwise. You'll have your own garage and repair shop, they say, you'll be able to live your dream.'

He had another attack of pain, and Spice waited for it to pass to let him talk, never trying to convince him that he'd get better. She had learned that for some people, acceptance was more important than false hope. He managed to talk for another ten minutes, though his face was drained of colour.

As she prepared to leave, she wondered if she had been any help, or whether her visit, and the strain of talking, had caused him more pain. It had been a battle for him. The answer came immediately.

'You don't know how important this has been for me,' he said. A single tear rolled down his cheek. 'Your being here, accepting me, accepting the situation I'm in, a dog talking to me as if you really understand. It seems a little unreal, but I know now that we are all part of one big design, people, animals, every living thing, a part of God's plan.'

After these two visits, Spice was able to tell the family that she understood the reason for her being sick with the parvovirus. 'It was a message,' she said. 'I needed to understand sickness so I could help others who are sick.'

'It's very good of you to have done that,' Scott told her. 'But I'm not convinced that you needed to suffer like you did to better understand sick people.'

'You've always had a gift of making people feel comfortable with you,' Tom added. He was thinking that the visits were a wonderful idea.

'I hope it's not making you too sad,' Tiffany showed her concern. 'I couldn't do it.'

'But what do the people you visit think about you being there?' Lara asked before Spice had time to answer.

'I really think it's doing them some good,' Spice said. 'It's early days yet, but I think Mavis and Tony were pleased that I saw them. And I learned a lot. I have ideas about many other things I can do, but the visits will be a big part of what I intend to do from now on.

Chapter 7

'This might be a good spot for afternoon tea,' Bill Wright said, taking off the haversack that was carrying the thermos and slices his wife Lyn had baked.

'It's so pretty,' Tina Haddon added, from the side of the riverbed where they'd stopped, and were looking at the surrounding bush. 'What do you think girls?'

The two Haddon girls, Olivia and Charlotte, one in her final year of primary school, and the other in her first year of secondary school, nodded. The two sons of Bill and Lyn Wright had nothing to say. Afternoon tea had more attraction for them than admiring the bush.

The Haddons and Wrights were long-standing friends and neighbours. They were to stay the night at the Hydro Majestic at Medlow Bath, and apart from some shopping at Leura and Katoomba, were to take some bush walks. Tina was a keen bush-walker, used to walking many kilometres, but they'd agreed not to venture too far, as it probably wasn't what the children would enjoy the most. They'd want to play and explore.

Today they had planned an afternoon walk, driving to Blackheath and climbing down the well-worn track from Govetts Leap. They had no particular destination in mind. They would walk for an hour and a half, which they had already done, then return. July was still winter, and they knew the sun would disappear behind the mountains by four o'clock. It would be dark not long after five.

There were rocks that were comfortable to sit on along the side of the small creek where they'd stopped. They could hear the trickle of the water and a thousand bush sounds of insects and birds. The sun slanted through the trees making everything around them look to be in brilliant colour.

Lyn and Tina took the afternoon tea things from the haversack, handed the children their juice, and poured the coffee. The two Wright brothers bolted their cake and juice.

'This is the life,' Graham Haddon said. It was a comment that most children had heard their parents say at some time or other, a comment that meant everything was good with the world. 'And when we get back, we can look forward to the fire in the dining room at the Hydro,' Bill added. 'And perhaps a brandy after dinner.'

Apart from the two boys, they were slow over their afternoon tea. Each of them was getting drunk on the sounds and sights of the bush. Each of them had retreated into their own private world, alone with their thoughts.

After ten minutes of near silence, Bill was the first to speak. 'I'm afraid it's time to head back,' he said with regret. 'We don't want to be caught in the dark.' He began to collect the cups and plates.

'Where are the boys?' Lyn said suddenly. The loudness and urgency of her voice seemed to fracture the dream-like quality of their thoughts.

'They were here not so long ago,' one of the Haddon girls said.

'Boys!' Lyn yelled. 'Steve! Mikey!' Her concern was spread across her face like a shadow. There was no answer. If anything had happened to one of the boys, they were a long way from help.

'They can't have gone far.' Bill wasn't too worried. 'I'll run along the track.'

He set off as Lyn continued to call, now looking very upset. And a minute later, they heard Bill calling from some distance away.

'I'll go back the other way,' Graham said. He felt helpless, but wanted to do something, so he began to retrace the way they had come. Tina began to call, and the two girls tried to comfort Lyn. 'I'm sure they'll be alright Mrs Wright,' one of them said, hoping it didn't sound too hollow.

Bill returned twenty minutes later, and he was concerned now. The sun was disappearing behind the mountains, and it would be dark in an hour. Lyn was crying, and Tina was holding her.

'Leave the red towel here,' Bill told Lyn, 'so if searchers are needed, they'll…' He saw Lyn's face and left the rest unsaid. 'You start going back,' he said to them all. 'I'll follow when I've called the police. And I'll wait for twenty minutes in case the boys find their way back.'

'I'm not going to leave here, while my boys…' Lyn protested, but was convinced by Tina that Bill's suggestion was the best plan to follow.

The day that had started so well was full of pain. Tina held on to Lyn as they walked back to join Graham. Olivia and Charlotte followed. 'It'll be night soon,' Lyn cried. 'What will they do? They could fall off a cliff and be killed. It'll be freezing. Those pullovers won't give them nearly enough warmth. Mikey will be so scared.'

Bill was lucky to reach the police straight away on his mobile, and when they all reached the top of Govetts Leap an hour later in the fading light, a small group of men was already waiting for them.

'People often lose their way,' one of two men with flashlights told them. They asked Bill where the boys had gone missing, and Bill was able to describe the spot marked by a red towel. He was a good judge of distances, and one of the men seemed to know the exact spot. 'Their names and ages?' the same man asked, as they prepared to start searching.

'Steve is ten. Mikey is nine. They both have blond hair and blue eyes,' Lyn needed to feel part of the rescue operation. 'They're very much alike, two peas in a pod, people say,' and she couldn't say any more. She didn't have to.

The two men set off, half running to make the most of the fading light.

'We usually tell people now to go back to their house or motel,' a kind policeman said. 'Because there's nothing they can do. But they always stay.'

'We're not going anywhere,' Bill replied, speaking for Lyn as well.

'We'll stay too,' Tina added, and she put her arm around Lyn's shoulders.

'What do you think the chances are?' Graham asked one of the two policemen, and wished he hadn't. It wasn't very thoughtful.

'They'll find them.' The answer was immediate. This wasn't an unusual event for them.

A couple of hours dragged by. Tina and Graham tried to comfort the Wrights, saying they were sure to come back safely, trying to make their voices sound cheerful. They were hugging themselves and stamping on the ground to keep warm. The two girls sat in the car and were silent, sensing the danger.

After what seemed an eternity, they saw the two flashlights coming towards them in the blackness. Bill and Graham ran towards them.

*

It was unusual for the Ellis family to watch television in the morning. Tom, Beth and Scott were always in a hurry to get to work, and Lara had a full day at university. Spice was going to a hospital. The word had spread about her visits to seriously sick patients, and she now received many requests to visit. Sometimes the requests came from hospital administrators once they had seen how at ease the visits made the patients. And often it was the patients themselves, or their families who wanted her to visit.

Some of the patients she had visited in the last few months had died. Tony Gianappolous had passed away, and Spice had received a wonderful letter from his family and another from Tina saying how grateful they were, and what a difference she had made to Tony's spirits. He had faced the end with bravery and dignity.

The family heard the news of the missing boys on the radio. Scott always had the alarm on the clock radio awaken him at 6.30 am, and the news followed. The story about lost boys was the first news item, and when he told the family, they turned on the television and watched as they dressed or had breakfast.

'Two brothers, aged nine and ten disappeared from a family outing near Govetts Leap in the Blue Mountains late yesterday afternoon. A search by two officers from the Police Rescue Squad, experienced in locating people lost in the mountains failed to find the two boys even though the place from which they departed had been clearly marked. The search was abandoned at night as police considered it too dangerous to continue. Grave fears are held for the two boys who must have spent the night in freezing conditions. Mr and Mrs Bill Wright from Kenthurst say that the two boys have no experience of how to survive in such conditions.'

The news coverage showed Bill and Lyn being comforted by police at the top of Govetts Leap. Lyn was holding a toy soldier. 'It's Mikey's favourite,' she told the camera. 'He hardly ever goes anywhere without it.'

'The search will resume at first light. Sergeant Randall will be coordinating the search effort, and already several Blackheath residents who know the area well have volunteered to help.'

Sergeant Randall didn't want to detail his plan for the search, as if it was a national secret, but he said what his television viewers would expect him to say, that he had every hope the two boys would be found safe and well.

'Poor parents,' Beth said. 'It's hard to imagine what they might be feeling now,' and she finished the last mouthful of her coffee.

'They'll find them,' Tom added, pointing to the police officers on the television screen. 'Unless of course they've fallen in the night. Let's just hope they sat down when it got dark, and they didn't try to walk around.'

Spice was the last to leave the house. The television coverage showed a police dog, a German shepherd with his handler. Good, Spice thought. The dog should be able to pick up the scent and lead the searchers to the boys. She smiled. This was one area where dogs were superior to people. They were specially trained to pick up human scent.

*

When they'd finished their afternoon tea, Steve and Mikey had wandered further down the track until they came to another stream. They'd decided to follow the stream rather than the track to see if there was a waterfall. They thought they could hear the roaring of water. The river seemed to be rushing by quickly. But after a short distance the stream ended.

They'd become confused and lost their way returning to the track, but had kept walking even when they realised they didn't know which way was the right way. Rather than stop, they were moving further away from the others.

'I'm scared,' Mikey told his brother who had taken the lead. 'Do you know where you're going. I think we might be going around in circles. Haven't we seen that fallen tree before?'

Steve was scared too, more frightened than he'd ever been, but he wasn't going to tell Mikey that.

They both thought they heard someone yelling, but it was a long way away, and they had different ideas as to where the sound came from. They both started to shout, and after a minute or two they took it in turns, and continued until they had no voice left. The bush seemed to swallow up their shouts.

It was not yet dark, but the sun was already retreating behind the mountains.

'What'll we do?' Mikey said.

Steve didn't answer and started to walk up a rise. He knew they'd walked down a long way from Govetts Leap, and thought the better way to go was up. He didn't have any idea how big an area the Blue Mountains was. This was the first time he'd seen them. Mikey hurried after him.

As it became darker, and they reached the top of a hill, they saw the bush spread out before them almost without end to a fuzzy light purple horizon a long way off. They knew they were nowhere near where they'd started. They'd been walking for two hours.

'I'm tired,' Mikey said. 'My feet hurt. It's getting cold.'

They huddled together, sitting on the ground. Mikey didn't have to be told there was no point in walking further. It was getting darker and they wouldn't be able to see where they were going. They both knew there were steep cliffs they could easily fall over.

'Dad will be furious,' Mikey said. 'Do you think he'll be looking for us?'

'Mum will be out of her mind with worry,' Steve added without answering Mikey's question. As the older of the two boys, he felt responsible.

The night was bitterly cold, and they lay down on the ground, covering each other with leaves. But it didn't stop their shivering. Steve found a biscuit he'd put in his pocket at lunchtime, and broke it in half. They slept in fits and starts. The ground was hard and they couldn't avoid the stones that bit into their bodies.

It was still freezing when the sky paled with morning. 'What'll we do?' Mikey asked. They didn't need to tell each other how cold and hungry they were. 'Did you have those lessons on bush tucker with Mrs Wilson?' he asked, and Steve shook his head.

Steve didn't know what to do. Part of him said it would be better to stay where they were. That was the sensible part. Another part of him cried out that they should be doing something, anything, and not just sitting around.

*

The Ellis family watched the television news on the second evening of the boy's disappearance. Sergeant Randall was interviewed and seemed less certain than he had been the evening before.

'We've had thirty searchers, police and local volunteers who know these parts well, looking for the boys. We think the police dogs picked up a scent where the boys left their parents, but they lost it. It is of great concern that the boys will have to spend another night in the bitter cold, but we will resume the search at first light in the morning. We have the services of two helicopters that will see what they can spot from the air.'

The television pictures showed weary searchers returning to the top of Govetts Leap, a police dog straining on its lead, and Bill and Lyn Wright holding each other and looking very distressed. The television interviewer didn't approach them out of respect. There were several onlookers who were kept behind a blue and white ribbon stretched between two trees.

'I know how I would feel if that were you when you were nine and ten,' Beth said, and she nodded to Scott and Lara. 'Those poor parents. It's not looking very promising is it?'

Tom remained silent. He simply shook his head. His confidence of the evening before had disappeared.

Spice was also silent and deep in thought. 'I think I can help,' she finally said. Tom and Beth looked at her. 'I know I can help,' she said with more emphasis.

'But what can you do Spice?' Tom asked. 'The police dogs lost the scent. Can you do anything that they can't do?'

'They have good tracking skills,' Spice replied. 'But they don't think like I do.'

'But how can you help?' Beth repeated Tom's question after a long pause. 'Is it some sixth sense that you have?'

'Could you take me to Blackheath?' Spice answered without replying to the question both Tom and Beth had asked. 'Let me talk to Sergeant Randall.'

Tom and Beth looked at each other. They knew that if Spice said something, she really meant it. Tom didn't want to say that Sergeant Randall would probably not want to have anything to do with them. But they decided that Beth would drive Spice to Blackheath immediately. That would mean she'd have to take the following day off work. They left in half an hour, taking enough belongings to stay the night in a motel.

It was a ninety-minute drive to Blackheath but the lights of the police station were still on, and Sergeant Randall and a small team of men were discussing search details for the following day. They were surprised rather than annoyed when Beth and Spice were introduced by the police officer at the front desk.

Like Tom, Beth thought they would meet a lot of opposition from the men. Who would want a woman with a small talking dog to have a say in how they conducted their search. But two of them had seen Spice on Australia's Got Talent, and they'd all seen the media reports about Spice, so they didn't mind hearing what she had to say.

Spice went straight to the map that was spread out on the table, stood on a chair and asked Randall where the boys had gone missing, where the dogs had started the search and lost the scent, and what ground the search had covered. She studied the map for a couple of minutes. It was a detailed map with contours that showed the height and steepness of all the mountains.

'If you would let me take a map like this one, and a mobile phone, I'd like to be part of your search tomorrow,' Spice said.

Of course, Randall didn't mind. The more searchers the better. He had dogs of his own, and knew that they had special powers, but they didn't have the near-human intelligence of Spice. 'Do you have an idea where they might be?' he asked, treating Spice as an equal. 'Is there something you'd like to share with us.'

'I do have an idea where they might have gone,' Spice answered. 'But it may be best if I follow my idea, and you continue with the search that you've planned so thoroughly.' Randall was happy with that, believing that he had all the answers. She later told Beth in their motel room that she thought Randall was searching in the wrong place.

The following morning, the searchers met at the top of Govetts Leap at first light. Bill and Lyn Wright were there looking terrible. They were grey and exhausted, but were pleased to see the famous dog had joined the search effort. It gave them a little flicker of hope.

After Spice had exchanged a few words with Bill and Lyn, she was taken to the place where the boys disappeared, and set off on her own with a map, a mobile phone and some water.

'Report in every hour or two,' Randall had told her. He believed his own searchers had the better chance of finding the boys, but when he saw Spice's determination, he began to have more faith in this miracle dog.

Spice could move more quickly through the bush than most people. It wasn't so much the boy's scent that guided her. It was more an instinct. Several times she would reach a spot, stand still as if she were sniffing the air, and consider which way to go. Even she wasn't sure what made her settle on a particular direction. Twice she heard the sound of helicopters a long way off.

She covered many kilometres before the sun was directly overhead. She sat down for only as long as it took her to have her first drink of water. The sky was blue and the coldness of the early morning was now the heat of midday. She had carried a mental picture of the map in her mind, but needed to look at it again. She called Randall to find that his searchers hadn't been successful either.

It was early afternoon when she found them. They were sitting with their backs to a large tree, looking pale and dirty. They were exhausted but were still able to show surprise and pleasure when a pretty cocker spaniel appeared from nowhere. They recognised Spice as the famous talking dog, and began to feel hope when they thought all had gone.

They were grateful for the water that Spice had left in her canteen, and asked her about their parents. They even seemed surprised that people might be out searching for them, as if no one might bother to do so. When asked if they were strong enough to walk, Steve said he was, and Mikey said he wasn't. It was obvious to Spice that neither of them could manage the walk back.

She spread the map on the ground and was able to identify exactly where they were. So, she used her mobile to phone the map coordinates to Randall so the boys could be easily located, and helped to return. She reported that the boys were hungry and exhausted but otherwise unharmed. The news of the boy's discovery was quickly reported to Bill and Lyn, and to the press. Minutes later as the boys waited for the rescuers, they were able to use Spice's mobile to talk to their parents. And Bill and Lyn Wright insisted on talking to Spice, saying through their sobbing that they would never be able to thank her enough.

The day was closing in by the time Spice and the rescuers returned carrying the boys. Mikey was being piggy-backed by a rescuer, and Steve insisted on walking the last few hundred metres. They were rushed by their tearful parents. Television cameras and reporters were there to capture the return. The

Australian public loved survival and good-luck stories like this. The boy's disappearance had captured the public imagination.

After questioning the boys to make sure they were alright, Bill and Lyn knelt to hug Spice, telling her they would be grateful to their dying days. They knew from Randall that she had found the boys. 'I'm so glad it's a happy ending,' Spice told them. 'They're nice boys, very respectful.' She almost asked them not to be too upset with the boys for wandering away, but she knew they wouldn't be.

She was then circled by the television reporters who competed with each other in asking questions. 'Where did you find them?' 'What condition were they in?' 'What was the first thing they said to you?' 'How did you know where to look?' 'How does it feel to have worked out where the boys were all by yourself?' one of them asked, and she was given the chance to answer.

'It wasn't all by myself,' Spice answered politely. 'It was all made possible by Sergeant Randall of the Blackheath Police. He's the one who should be given all the credit.' Even as she said it, she could see Randall's grateful nod and smile. He was waiting his turn to be interviewed.

Spice continued to be given credit for the rescue, and each time she insisted that Sergeant Randall was the real hero. She wasn't happy being called a heroine and avoided giving interviews when she thought the interviewer only wanted to give her praise, and not ask about the more important issues like looking after children, and how to survive in the bush.

'How did you know where to look?' Beth asked her on the way home that night. But Spice wasn't even sure how she knew. She just knew.

'You know Spice, that every time someone goes missing in the Blue Mountains from now on, which is every week, the police will come running to you to help.' Spice just smiled.

'Well,' Beth added a few minutes later, 'let Sergeant Randall be the hero of the people. But you're our hero!'

Chapter 8

On two occasions over the next year, Spice was called on to help rescue people who had been lost in the Blue mountains. One was an experienced single male walker visiting from another country, and the other was an inexperienced group of four. She was able to locate them with little effort. There were many other rescues but all were carried out successfully without Spice's help.

She continued with her work visiting the seriously ill in hospitals and family homes, and was invited to sit on a number of committees that examined how to look after the aged and seriously ill, and how to achieve better and more equal living conditions for everyone. It was widely thought that having the opinion of a non-person might be valuable. Spice argued that people from all disadvantaged groups should be on these committees.

Tom and Beth continued working and enjoyed popularity and promotion. Tom was now a deputy principal in a school. Beth remained assistant to the boss and had turned down the position of running another branch of the company, saying she preferred to work with Bruce Dalton. She never missed the opportunity to walk or run with Spice each night.

Lara was ending her training to be a vet, and was at the top of her year of graduating students. She had received a lot of help from Spice in understanding the medical condition of animals, and what they thought about being sick. Scott had announced his engagement to marry Tiffany.

One Saturday morning towards the end of Spring, Spice called for a family conference. She knew what she had to say would shock the family so she didn't want a hurried meeting in the evening. She hadn't called a family meeting before so the family was a little anxious. How do you say you are leaving when you love your life, and you love the people who have made that life so happy? The family and Tiffany waited in silence.

'You must know how I feel about you all,' she began. 'Ever since I knocked on your door dripping wet from the storm, you took me in, cared for me and loved me. You always wanted what was best for me.' The family was watching her closely now. Each one of them sensed that something very significant was about to be said, and they were concerned.

'I've decided to go overseas.' She hurried on before someone could protest. 'I'll miss you all terribly, but I need to work with the dogs over there.' It was said. She had been worried for days about having to say it.

The family was shocked. It was a complete surprise. Beth was the first to speak. If it was a short trip, she might be able to visit on her holidays. 'How long will you be away?' she asked.

'It isn't just a trip like a holiday,' Spice answered, not wanting to look directly at Beth.

It slowly dawned on the family that Spice might be leaving them forever.

'But there's so much to be done here.' Beth was very upset. 'Why can't you help, or work with the dogs here, whatever you do, rather than the ones that are thousands of kilometres away.'

Spice moved across to Beth, and took her arm. 'I've already helped the dogs here. There's not much more I can do.' After a pause, she said quietly, 'I've given it a lot of thought. Sometimes there are things we might be afraid of doing, but we have to do them. It's something I have to do.'

Tom was also upset. Like every member of the family, he loved Spice, and her leaving would make a big emptiness in their lives. He was also reminded painfully of his meeting with Donegal years ago, when even with their joking, Donegal had said he needed to help other dogs. Donegal was lost to him from that time, and had never talked or walked upright again. He knew how determined Donegal had been, and he had no reason to believe that Spice would be any different. He would not stand in her way.

Tiffany, who had been very close to Spice from the beginning, was disappointed, but accepted her decision, and moved to hug her. 'I'll expect an email at least two or three times a week,' she said.

Scott and Lara were shocked. There had been no warning, no suggestion of what Spice must have been thinking for months. 'It's almost like a death in the family,' Lara thought to herself. But she had a 'steady' boyfriend in Eric, and Scott was marrying Tiffany.

'Make sure you don't go before the wedding,' Scott was joking, trying to ease the pain of the meeting, but the pain still lingered in the air.

*

Spice chose a date in January, a few months away for her departure. The thought of flying scared her. She'd never been in a plane before. 'Dogs like to have their feet firmly on the ground,' she joked, and there were stories of some dogs having breathing problems in planes. There was one small hiccup. No airline would allow her to travel alone. As an animal, even a half-human one, she was required to be the responsibility of a human. That would mean one of the family would have to fly to Heathrow airport in London, see that she was safe, and return almost as soon as they arrived there.

Tom and Beth discussed who should go with her. Beth was probably the closest to Spice, so Tom was surprised when she asked him if he would go.

'Why?' he asked. 'I don't understand.'

'I'd like to say my final goodbyes here,' Beth answered, and her eyes were watering. 'That plane trip all the way there, and all the way back…alone…' She didn't have to explain anymore. 'Besides, you'll be free. It will still be school holidays.'

'There's one thing I'd really like you to do for me,' Spice told them a few days after the conference when the family was starting to accept her decision. 'I'd like to have a dinner party with four of my friends, and with all of you of course. I think it's important you see and talk to them. It may help you to understand.'

At the mention of the word 'talk', the family looked at her in amazement, but didn't say anything. The thought that there might be other talking dogs was a cause for wonder, but they'd grown used to surprises. 'You'll see what I mean,' she added.

The family with Spice's help spent a week preparing for the dinner. 'There's six of us, if we include Tiffany and Spice, and four dogs. That makes ten,' Tom said his thoughts aloud. 'Do you think ten of us can squeeze around the table?'

'I think Spice wants us all to sit at the table,' Beth answered. 'She hasn't said anything about them sitting like people, she hasn't said anything about them talking to us, but when she talks of a dinner party, I don't think she means a bowl of kibble or a few raw bones thrown on the lawn outside.'

'Should we ask her?' Tom said quietly.

'No!' Beth replied. 'That might hurt her feelings. I think we can assume that we'll all be at the table. And I think we can assume that these friends of hers will all have special talents.'

Armed with Spice's advice, they decided on a meal of beef and baked vegetables followed by a peach pie. They rejected the chocolate mousse because they'd heard that too much chocolate was bad for dogs.

'Can you tell us something about our four dinner guests?' Tom asked.

'They're all different,' Spice answered, so there'll need to be a pile of cushions on one chair for Curly. She's a poodle and is even shorter than me. The others will all be fine. Toby is an Irish Wolfhound, and his breed is the tallest of all dogs. Rocky is a boxer, and while he's heavy, he's not as tall as Toby. Princess is a Labrador, and Curly is a poodle. They are the names people have given them. We call ourselves by different dog names.

The excitement increased in the Ellis house as the day approached. 'If they're all sitting at the table, does that mean they can talk?' Lara asked. 'If they're all sitting at the table, does that mean they can use a knife, fork and spoon?' Scott added. 'Does it mean that their table manners are as good as Donegal's and Spice's?'

'I can't wait,' Tiffany said. She had been very close to both Donegal and Spice, and the thought of there being other dogs like them made her giddy with excitement.

When the evening came, the dogs arrived together, and Spice welcomed them at the door to introduce them to each member of the family. Each dog was standing upright, and reached out its paw without any shyness. Toby even bowed from his great height. 'I've heard so much about you,' each of them said. 'It's a pleasure to meet you.' Lara's question as to whether they could talk had been answered, though Spice had already suggested that they could.

Toby was very tall with spikey grey hair and a pleasant but non-smiling face. He walked in with an air of importance, and spoke with a slow and deep voice that fitted his size. Rocky was solid and tan coloured with sparkling eyes and a smile on his face that remained that way throughout the evening. He entered as if he'd lived with the Ellis family his whole life, and spoke quickly as though all of life was an exciting adventure. Prince was an attractive honey-coloured Labrador and seemed to be a little more reserved than the others. She spoke softly and very precisely as if she had carefully considered each comment. Curly was a small white poodle who looked around the house with great curiosity. She spoke, taking a great interest in the answers to her questions.

'Something smells good.' Rocky was the first to speak once the introductions were complete. 'I'm starving. Oh, I beg your pardon Beth,' he added. 'I hope that didn't seem rude.'

They were already using first names, and it was apparent that the dogs had been given information about each of the family members. They decided not to have pre-dinner drinks, and went straight to the table instead, where Spice had put place names to indicate where each person was to sit. There was a member of the family between each dog. Rocky, who was placed next to Tiffany, pulled out her chair for her to sit. Toby did the same for Lara.

There were no awkward silences. Beth served the meal, and the conversation flowed.

'We want to hear all about each of you,' Beth said, and Spice, knowing that her guests would be too humble to talk about their talents, started with a more detailed introduction of each of them.

'Toby is our athlete, and he is very strong. He could fight if he needed to, but he hasn't felt the need yet.'

'There are other ways of fighting rather than just using your physical strength,' Toby added in his deep voice. 'I'll fight for what is just, but using strength of a different kind. I want to help all the people and animals who are not treated well.'

'Rocky is a wonderful public speaker,' Spice continued her introductions. 'He knows how to make an audience listen, and can be very persuasive.'

'We need to be able to argue for everyone, animals included, to be equal', Rocky said, having put down his fork, finished a mouthful, and used the napkin to wipe his mouth. 'I want the same as Toby, and we can help each other to achieve it.'

'Do you want to tell them what your talents are Princess?' Spice asked, feeling that she was going too far in directing the flow of talk.

'This meal is delicious Beth,' Princess answered. 'You must have gone to so much trouble.' She paused and continued. 'My particular interest is Astrophysics. Other dogs want to know what it is. Most people don't know. It's a branch of science that applies the laws of physics to explain the stars and planets.'

'But why would a dog...' Scott began. 'Oh, I'm sorry Princess, that sounded rude.'

'It's alright Scott,' Princess was quick to reply. 'Why would a dog be interested? I suppose I could answer by saying why would people be interested. I think it's important we understand as much about the world, even the world beyond our own planet, as we can. I want to contribute to that understanding.'

'Can you wait a minute Curly while I get the sweets,' Beth said. 'I don't want to miss any of this,' and she headed for the kitchen. Lara followed to help.

'Aren't they wonderful?' Lara whispered to Beth.

'I can hardly believe it,' Beth answered. 'They're so polite, so well mannered, so ... so caring about the world.'

'How did you know peach pie was my favourite,' Curly began as the sweets were served and the dogs waited for Beth to sit. 'I think I know,' and she looked at Spice and smiled. 'My interest is history. I want to recall and interpret the past so that it makes sense to people now.'

'And we don't keep making the same mistakes,' Rocky added.

'Curly has a photographic memory,' Spice explained. 'She can remember everything she's read and everything she hears. That has to be rather helpful for anyone who writes history.'

The conversation continued long into the night. They all discussed what they believed were the big problems in the world today, and what could be done about them. The family was particularly interested in details of how their guests could help. The dogs also showed a strong interest in each family member, and rather than 'hold the floor' with their own talk, asked for their opinions with genuine interest, even though they had been thoroughly 'briefed' by Spice.

When it was time to go, each of the dogs thanked the family for having them and swore the family to secrecy. They didn't want people to know just yet what they could do, and what they planned to do. That hadn't been settled yet. They gave the family details of how they could be contacted, and once they'd walked upright out the front door, they raced away on all four feet like any ordinary dog.

The family sat down together an hour later once the cleaning-up was complete. It was after midnight, but no one wanted to go to bed. They couldn't sleep if they tried. The appearance of Donegal, and years later Spice, were miracles, but four dogs all at once was hard to comprehend! So, they sat together in the family room, and each of them knew that Spice would want to know what they thought of her very special friends.

'Wow,' was all Scott could say. There was a long silence.

'Weren't they terrific,' Tiffany added. 'So clever, so charming.'

'I don't know what I'm feeling right now,' Lara remarked. 'I feel so happy to have met them, and I feel sad that they are dogs, and most people don't treat them with much respect.' There was another long silence.

'Thank you Spice,' Beth said, her voice cracking with emotion. 'I understand now why you introduced us to your friends. And while I'm not looking forward to your leaving us, now that I've seen Toby and Rocky and Princess and Curly, I understand why you have to go. If you can do over there what you have achieved here…'

'It's not all my doing Beth,' Spice was quick to explain. 'Donegal and I simply helped to bring out what is best in each of our friends.'

Spice knew that the family understood, and there was no need for her to explain any further. She thanked Tom and Beth as her guests had done, hugged them all, and went to her room.

*

Spring soon became summer. Spice continued with her hospital visits and her committee work. Nothing changed in the family routine.

They had Spice's four friends to dinner again in November, and they shared Christmas together. The four dogs became friendly with each family member. Tom went running after their November dinner with Toby and found that he could run even faster than Donegal. Scott was no match for the powerful Rocky when they wrestled on the back lawn, taking care that no one apart from the family was watching. Beth and Tiffany spent time in the lounge room discussing

Astrophysics with Princess, wanting to know how it could change the world for the better. Lara, and Tom, who taught history at school, tried to convince Curly to write a history of how dogs became so intelligent, and wanted to know if there were talking cats and horses.

It was still a little painful to talk about Spice's departure, more so as the time was quickly approaching, but the visits from her four friends, and their promises to make frequent visits, made it easier to discuss. The more they talked about it, the easier it became to accept. 'We mustn't forget,' Tom told Beth, 'that they will miss her as much as we will.'

Spice was to leave the day after Scott and Tiffany's wedding. The family was surprised at how little preparation was needed for her departure. She wasn't taking anything. 'I suppose,' Beth said, 'it would look strange for a dog to be carrying big suitcases.'

'Everything I need will be waiting for me when I arrive,' Spice told them, and they wondered how she knew.

The wedding was a great occasion. It was held at a small church in Dural, and there was a reception in a grand home nearby. Spice of course attended and sat at the official table. Tiffany had given much thought as to whether Spice should be a bridesmaid, but decided against it. It might have looked odd, she certainly couldn't wear a dress to match those of the other bridesmaids, and she had to think of Scott's groomsman who would accompany her.

After the speeches she was called on to sing, the first time she had sung in public since Australia's Got Talent. She began with Adele's *Make You Feel My Love*, and finished with Elvis Presley's *Can't help Falling in Love With You.* Scott thanked her in his speech, saying how she'd been a wonderful friend both to Tiffany and to the family. He didn't mention her leaving. That had remained a family secret and would have meant a thousand questions that would be difficult to answer, and more attention from the media. The wedding guests had fallen under her spell, and danced long into the night. She did too.

The timing was good. The family was still feeling a glow the following day from the happiness of the wedding. Perhaps it would help lessen the sadness of Spice's departure. They gathered in the family room, and 'put on a brave face' as they took turns to say goodbye. Scott and Tiffany had said their emotional goodbyes the previous night before they set off on their honeymoon.

Lara said a few tearful words, holding both of Spice's paws. Most of what they all felt had been said in the last few months. Then it was Beth's turn. 'Don't say anything,' Beth, who had been rehearsing this moment for weeks, told her, and they hugged. There was no need to say what they felt and what they meant to each other.

But there was still a sinking feeling, a feeling of emptiness and loss as they watched Tom driving away to the airport with Spice waving sadly from the car window. The house felt different when they went back inside, as if it had lost its soul.

The flight was uneventful except for the passengers pointing at Spice or coming to talk to her. She had not been forgotten. The airline had a strict policy about flying animals, but they agreed to make an exception and let Spice accompany Tom as long as he paid for the extra seat.

When they arrived at Heathrow airport in London, it was time for Tom to say goodbye. There was to be no stay in a motel. They hugged. For the people in London, it was curious seeing a man kneeling to hug a dog, but it was not that unusual to see a man showing affection for his pet. While there had been news coverage of the wonder dog in Australia, Spice was not as well known in England.

There was no one to meet her, at least not inside the airport. Any dog or group of dogs waiting for the passengers to exit through customs would have been shooed away. So, with their goodbyes finished, Spice simply darted away on all four feet like any other dog, without turning to look back.

Tom had been prepared for this goodbye, but it didn't stop the feeling of loss. He only had to wait a couple of hours for the long return flight. It was enough time for him to wash and shave in the airport restroom, and to buy a cup of coffee and a donut in the airport lounge.

It was when he'd boarded and the plane raced down the runway and climbed into the air, that everything seemed so final. Until then, it had all seemed half real.

Tom watched from his window seat as his flight circled to return to Australia and home. He saw from thirty thousand feet in the air the mass of houses like a toy city below him, containing the millions of lives, each with their own joys and pains, the million different dreams, and he thought of Spice and Donegal. He couldn't wait to return to the comfort of his own home. And he couldn't help think what a strange, rich, bitter-sweet and rewarding world we live in.